FA

"Don't lie to me," Leslie said, standing close. "What's your grudge, boy? It's something personal, isn't it? Something between us?" He stood silent for a moment, looking into Lee's face. "Did I kill someone you knew?" There was a wry twist to his mouth. " . . . A member of your family?"

"Yes!" It had burst out of Lee Morgan like water from a broken pot. "You damn sure did kill someone I knew! A member of my family. You killed my mother—you dirty son-of-a-bitch!" The Remington was out again, and in the boy's hand, and it shook like an aspen leaf.

Leslie took a step back. "I never shot a woman in my life."

"You didn't shoot her." Lee's voice was shaking as much as the pistol. "It would have been better if you had shot her—better than leaving her alone till she couldn't stand it anymore!"

"Who the hell are you talking about, boy?"

"My mother, that's who. *Beatrice Morgan.*"

Frank Leslie had never been hit harder—not by any bullet that had struck him, or by any horse kick, either. He was seeing other mountains in other country . . . a whorehouse . . . a thin, dark-eyed prostitute . . . and then the shooting that set him on his way again, wandering.

"I didn't know," Buckskin Frank Leslie said to his son. "She never told me she was carrying. And there were good reasons, damn good reasons, for my going."

Lee Morgan's face went white. The big Remington steadied, the muzzle leveled at Leslie's heart.

Also in the Buckskin Series:

BUCKSKIN #1: RIFLE RIVER
BUCKSKIN #2: GUNSTOCK
BUCKSKIN #3: PISTOLTOWN
BUCKSKIN #4: COLT CREEK
BUCKSKIN #5: GUNSIGHT GAP
BUCKSKIN #7: CARTRIDGE COAST
BUCKSKIN #8: HANGFIRE HILL
BUCKSKIN #9: CROSSFIRE COUNTRY
BUCKSKIN #10: BOLT-ACTION
BUCKSKIN #11: TRIGGER GUARD
BUCKSKIN #12: RECOIL

BUCKSKIN #6

TRIGGER SPRING

ROY LEBEAU

LEISURE BOOKS  NEW YORK CITY

A LEISURE BOOK®

September 2003

Published by

Dorchester Publishing Co., Inc.
200 Madison Avenue
New York, NY 10016

ISBN 0-8439-2229-X

Printed in the United States of America.

Visit us on the web at www.dorchesterpub.com.

CHAPTER ONE

THEY CAME from all the West there was. From the Bravo and the Trinity, the Green and the Missouri, and Columbia and the Red. They rode in from mountain range and cattle range, from mining town and cow town, from saloon and brothel, from lumber camps and camp meetings. Mostly men, but a few women among them. A boy or two.

Some came with a possible killing on their minds. Some not. And some, press men and reporters for the big city papers, scriveners and limners, came to view the spot, to take Brady's of it, to sketch it for Harpers, for another of the Eastern monthlies.

The spot—a hotel restaurant, really, something elegant for such a small town buried deep in the high mountains.

Grover was the name of the town.

The Grover House, name of the hotel.

There, right in there, Buckskin Frank Leslie—yes sir, that man himself (one of the old-timey jim dandies, by God!) had come to life, risen out of the past, out of legend, and here and now, nearly a decade short of the turn of the century, had shot the living innards out of Frank Pace, the Texas Plague, the Prairie Doom himself.

Right in there.

And then was shot in the back (the back, sir!) by nothing but a dirty whore, and killed.

Or as near as made no difference.

A life out of legends, sir. Worthy of the Illiad, or at least the Odyssey.

Finished, now. A slug, they say, clipped a chunk from the man's backbone; so he lies, unable to walk, barely able to lift a hand and that damn slowly, to show he needs the chamber pot. Dying, the Doc says, by slow degrees. And kept company by that woman —the Catherine whore, the rougher ladies call her, who bought a horse ranch, left her husband (a little Canadian cattle king) and moved Leslie and herself, too, with no apparent shame, into a ranch house to do god-knows-what in the months before the great gunman dies.

A sad story, sir. A sad end for a great fighting man. Betrayed twice by women, once to his death, once to dishonor.

Many men came to Grover, some women, too. A few boys.

Some of the men were fierce, and were not satisfied to stand in the hotel lobby, and stare at the dark stains in the fine oak flooring of the dining room. They desired a more complete satisfaction.

These men rode out of town, out and up into the highland meadows under the looming shadow of the Old Man, the first great peak, in that country, introducing the barrier of the Rockies. They rode over meadow and break, down the Little Chicken and across it, out and over the rolling miles of Broken Iron land, and so, even higher, to the horse ranch where Leslie lay, dying, to all accounts.

These men, for many various reasons, wished to see . . . to be certain sure.

Most of these men—and they were hard men, used to having their way against other hard and dangerous men—were stopped short of the ranch house. The adulterous woman—who had been a lady—Catherine Dowd, she had been, Catherine god-knew-what she was now, had hired a small crew of drovers to keep the place clear. She'd hired well. Six whang-leather riders, two old and gray and mean as snakes, four young randy gun-mad boys to back them up. And all fit to work like the horses they watched and doctored and herded and cared about.

A prime crew. More than enough to send most hard cases to the right-about. And did. Usually by grim words and grim looks. Occasionally by pointing Winchesters at them.

Sent most hard cases on their way, did the crew of the Spade Bit. Most, but not all.

They sent the Pinkerton men on their way, after some threats, and some offered frog-skin, and some pleading that they only wanted to measure the fellow, to Bert him for their files and records. To be certain sure . . .

The Pinkertons were turned back at the gate, and grumbled and turned to threaten again and were laughed at. Then they grumbled some more and climbed up into their buckboard and drove back the long way to Grover.

Many others were turned back as well, some not as easily as the Pinkertons had been. A tall man, two revolvers in his belt, rode cross country and down to headquarters and up to the corrals before the drovers caught him. There were words, and then there was trouble. The tall man shouted something about his dead brother, and then drew his weapons and ran for the house. Sid Sefton shot him down with a rifle so that he fell dying on the front step of the small log mainhouse, the revolvers still held in his hands. Catherine Dowd had come out of the house then, a small nickel-plated pistol in her left hand, and looked down at the dying man, then had put the nickel-plated pistol down on the porch planking, and took the dying man's head into her lap, becoming soaked with blood that instant, and asked why the poor fool had done it. The man could not answer, but blew slow bubbles of blood and died so. In her lap.

That way, the drovers knew that Catherine Dowd, in event of trouble, stood behind the door with her small pistol in her hand to protect the man slowly dying inside. Knowing this, they were doubly savage to keep any bad man from arriving at that door through them.

The six drovers loved Catherine Dowd, or grew to love her, as any decent man must, who lived beside a lovely and beleagered woman of great heart. In the Black Ace, where Spade Bit drank in Grover, no man called that lady a whore.

These six drovers stopped most of the pushing visitors to Spade Bit, and in late fall Bill Monk was killed doing it. Bill was one of the young ones, and wild and nasty as an Arkansas boar. George Peach heard shooting up by South Pond, and rode that way, and found Billy dead in a plaid drift of leaves, fallen just the night before from dwarf elms in a wind. Billy was shot twice and dead where he lay, his Colt held fast in his hand. One shot fired from it.

The drovers left their work and rode down the shooters' trail—there'd been two—but never came up to them.

Still, even if shorthanded now, the five were enough to win a dying man and his lady some freedom from being targets of revengeful men tracking Leslie to the last of his reputation, freedom from the curious, as well. But not perfect freedom.

Some men would not be stopped.

A marshal named LeFors came by, a short, pleasant looking man. He rode a tired bay to the main gate, sat it, waiting, and then—when two of the drovers arrived with rifles—smiled, waved a good morning to them, and rode on in and up the track to the house.

"You stop where you are, you son-of-a-bitch!" Bud Bent, while levering a shell into his carbine.

"I am a United States Marshal, son, LeFors my name." Back over his shoulder as he rode on by. "You go get you a good muley with that piece, I'll help you eat him."

In short, the man would not be stopped.

He rode up to the house, climbed down with a grunt, went up to the front door—a swift glance down to a dark stain on the steps—and knocked like a Christian.

He went in when Catherine Dowd allowed him, stayed for a very short time, and reappeared, blowing his nose in a light blue bandanna. Then he rode away.

A layman named Tilghman came by later—had ridden and railroaded a very long way. He had laughed with the drovers, and jollied them—and would not be stopped short of murder. He reminded them of Mister LeFors.

Bill Tilghman stood on the narrow porch for some time, his hat in his hand, talking to Catherine Dowd. Then he went inside.

The place was a common enough little three-room house, whitewashed and neat as a pin. The sort of house a lonely woman will clean and clean again through the long days. The furnishings were fine stuff, her own family stuff, Bill Tilghman thought.

She took him into the bedroom and he saw Frank Leslie lying there.

It was Frank, for sure. Tilghman had had doubts. The Leslie he'd known, now so many years ago, had seemed close to un-killable from sheer high spirits as much as that gun-skill of his, that made eyes pop at casual practice in some gully back of town.

But . . . but only a ghost of that man. A skeleton of him, dry and brown, lying there in a sleep as close as maybe to death itself. Hair gray as any grizzly. It looked like Buckskin Frank Leslie's daddy, or granddaddy, lying there.

It was a shock, and it reminded Tilghman of his own years forcefully. The dying man looked to be Father Time himself.

Tilghman made his apologies to the lady, asked if she needed help of any kind, and left. He was sorry he had come.

One other man the drovers passed—and a boy, later. They passed the man because they were afraid of him.

He came up the long road from town in late afternoon, as the first snow of winter was falling. The sun was shining as the light snow fell, which happens sometimes at the start of that season, and the countryside was blazing with light between blowing soft curtains of snow.

This man rode out of those curtains on a fat, rented hack, came to the gate. He'd been seen a mile out by Jay Clevenger and rode on through like a king. This man was tall and something plump, with a little snub nose and a spike mustache, and he had a clever, rolling eye. He was wearing a buffalo-robe coat big enough for two, but unbuttoned in the sunny chill to show a marvelous waistcoat, flowered in silk and stuff, with what seemed to be gold threads through it. The handle of a revolver of some make also peeped through the opened shaggy coat.

So, the fellow jogged along, and didn't pull up when three of the drovers, Clevenger and two others, drew up alongside. They spoke to him, but the fellow only glanced at them and rode on, and didn't answer. There'd been just enough sunshine snow by then that their horses left tracks along the way.

Clevenger, one of the old hands, had spurred up front to block the fellow's path, laid his pony across it, drew his Remington, and rested the pistol on his saddle-bow, full cocked. Clevenger sported great mustaches that end-drooped to his chin, he had a nose some chewed-on by a pox, and eyes as dark as flint. He had not always been a cowboy.

"Say, now," he said to this fat pilgrim on the hack. "That's as pretty a vest as I've seen, save on a pimp. You don't turn that pig and ride off Spade Bit, I'll see you're buried in it."

A wind blew a curtain of snow across them as he said it.

Whichever, it seemed to wake the fellow up, for he pulled in the hack, tilted back his hat—a hard hat like a dude's—stared hard at Clevenger, and said, "You have a loose lip, Mister, for a man who looks to have seen the elephant. Now, if you say one more word—any word at all—if you open your mouth even to breathe, then I'll kill you. And these two assholes to boot." And tilted his hat back down, kicked up the hack, and went on his way—which was where Clevenger sat.

Clevenger sat a moment more, and stared at the fellow as he came ambling.

Then he backed his horse out of the way. And didn't open his mouth to say a word, for he had seen weary death in the fellow's eyes.

The other two drovers did nothing either. They had never before seen Clevenger afraid.

"Now, who the hell was that?" Charlie Potts, nineteen years old, and tough enough to bet finger-joints in a barrelhouse, which he had done in Wyoming, and lost all the little finger of his left hand.

"I don't know," Clevenger said. "And I don't want to know. Now stop jawing and go ride around and tell Miz Dowd the fellow's coming."

"There's three of us, and we can stop him, whoever!" Sid Sefton, also nineteen.

"I don't think so," Clevenger said. "Now, ride!"

And away Sefton went, still believing himself immortal.

He beat the stranger to the ranch house by a good bit, knocked on the door, told Catherine Dowd about it, then stood, a brave boy, beside her, his hand on the butt of a small mail order revolver from Harrington and Richardson.

The stranger rode past the holding pen, and the smithy, and then, in a brilliant sunlight—the snow having quit—rode up to the porch and took off his hat to Mrs. Dowd. He had pleasant pale blue eyes, a perky nose like a large schoolgirl's. The bright waistcoat took her eye.

"Good afternoon, ma'am. Please allow me to introduce myself? I'm Ben Thompson, of Austin, Texas. And I've come on up here to have a word or two with Mister Leslie. I understand he is in that house."

Catherine Dowd was a woman of profoundly good sense. She took a long look at the man's face, his pleasant expression, and oddly pleased look in his eyes. She had seen that look before, or something like it, in the face of a merry madman come down to breakfast.

"Mister Leslie would be glad to meet you, sir, on any occasion if he were well."

"You're saying he is not? Is sick? Not skulking, is he?" The pleasant voice was slowly rising in pitch, the man was flushing pink. "Has the dog turned coward?" Up to an animal's howl. Mrs. Dowd smelled whiskey across the porch. Mister Thompson was drunk.

"I'll shut that mouth for you, Fatty!" Sid Sefton, off to the porch side, pulled at his revolver.

The world's time may then have continued as before; the time on the porch of headquarters' house on Spade Bit did not. There, time grew slow as setting mortar. It took Catherine a great deal of time to begin to open her mouth to speak. It took young Sefton even longer to draw his gun.

It took Ben Thompson no time at all to turn in his

saddle, flip the hairy coattail aside, draw a .45 caliber revolver from beside his waistcoat, cock it, aim it, and fire a single shot to break young Sidney's arm, as he, so slowly, tried to haul his pistol clear of leather.

The gunshot broke the spell.

The boy, his revolver spilling finally out of its holster to thump and clatter on the porch, spun half around and staggered into one of the supporting posts, his face as white as whey.

And Catherine, peering through gunsmoke, was able again to speak—and do more. She strode across the porch, to the rail, and leaning way over where Thompson sat his dopey stable hack, his revolver still nested comfortably in his hand, pulled back her own slimmer and more delicate one, and slapped him across his face so hard he lost his hat.

"Will you!" she cried. "Will you kill a boy—and my Frank?" And made to hit him again.

At which, Mister Thompson of Austin ducked away, reining the hack aside, and began to laugh, his face growing as red as it had before in anger. "Well hit!" he said, laughing. "And serve me right for rudeness." He put his pistol away, and suddenly and easily leaned down from the saddle to pick his hat up from the ground. "No more than I deserve for doubting a lady's word," he said, and waved away the two drovers, Clevenger and Potts come riding white-faced as English cows at the sound of the shot and the sight of Catherine Dowd in gun-smoke on her front porch.

"No trouble, boys," he called. "I've had my whipping." And turned back to her. "If Leslie ever gets well, tell him it's all square with Thompson. After all, there's hardly any of us good ones left." The hack sidled, nervous after the event. Thompson took off his hat to her. "Sorry about the boy there, ma'am. Fear I was somewhat the worse for drink . . . great pleasure meeting you . . . felicitations to Leslie, should he recover. You are a noble creature."

And with that, reined the hack away, and trotted on out of the ranch house yard, not looking back, not glancing at the two drovers sitting with their rifles across their saddle-bows.

As he'd turned, Catherine had seen the small print of her hand, still an angry red across his right cheek. She turned from that shaggy-coated back retreating, and went to help Sid Sefton, who was sitting on the porch edge in a faint, a bone of his broken arm poked snowy white through the soggy red of his checkered shirt sleeve.

Behind the closed house door, past the small neat parlor, the closed door of the tiny bedroom, Buckskin Frank Leslie lay dreaming of thunder.

Those three men, the drovers could not stop—the two lawmen with casual and determined ways, and that one gunman from Texas. All the others, though, they held away from Spade Bit, and did that while getting through their hard day's work. Of course, they could do nothing about men and women who came out in buggies and buckboards and stayed on the road outside Bit land, because that road ran over government free graze, and was open to anyone who didn't spook stock, or try to steal it. The drovers could do nothing about those people, who came driving out, and picnicing out there off the ranch land, hoping for a look at Catherine Dowd, who left her husband to nurse a famous killer with a bullet-broken back.

Those people could come out but they couldn't see her. Catherine stayed back at the house, back deep into her own land, almost a half-mile from the road, where no one could see her, and call out.

When she rode out, which she did seldom, she rode to the south—and further from the road.

As for the women—and there had been a few, coming to Grover with their men, or alone—only two of them tried to come out onto the ranch to see the adultress and her killer. One of these women was beautiful; she had come from a great hotel deep in the Rockies. This woman was stopped by the drovers at the gate, and being stopped, stood there to pray silently, then helped by Jay Clevenger she mounted her mare and rode away. The other woman was very different, a strong fat woman who was a writing reporter for the New York *Herald*. She also was stopped at the gate, by Charlie Potts, and had more than a few words to say to him. Charlie listened very politely to talk he'd never heard from a lady—the writing reporter was mighty angry—and had heard seldom from a whore, come to think about it. The fat lady said her say, got back in her buggy. Pop Beard had driven her out in a rented rig and she went on her way.

The next day, she rode cross-crountry to come to the ranch house that way. George Peach and Bud Bent caught her at the spring where the Little Chicken rose, and she was just as fortunate that Bent was there. George Peach was a violent boy, and odd.

The fat lady said her say to those two as well as she had at the gate the day before, but shorter. She must not have cared for the look of young George Peach. She finished that shorter say, and they whipped her hired pony up and sent her bucketing down the meadows headed for Grover at more than respectable speed. As far as anyone on the Bit knew, she didn't write a report on that to be printed in a New York paper.

These two, the beautiful one and the fat one, were the only two women who really tried to get up to the house. Other women, an imitation Calamity Jane or two, a silly girl, more than half a whore, who sang songs in saloons in town, and a woman preacher with messages from scripture. These sort of ladies did come to Grover, and stuck for a while, claiming to have known Leslie here or there, under this circumstance or that, claiming to have seen that killer and gunfighter in company with the cattle king's wife in Chicago years ago, in St. Louis . . . in Jacksonville, Florida, keeping company there with Wesley Hardin and his cousin.

They stuck but only for a while. The Calamity Janes finding Grover sadly flat, after a while, when no more shooting was offered—no serious shooting in any case—decamped, as did the lady preacher. The sort-of-a-whore hung on, singing for grub and dimes in the saloons and resorts, until to everyone's surprise she was taken on as wife by Edgar Pabst, who owned the biggest feed store in Grover, and should have known better. But the girl, though thin and not pretty, was young, and had a wildness about her. Strangeness. Slight mustache, too. Pabst seemed pleased enough, and so did she, sashaying around the better side of town in white dresses and a parasol with little silk tea roses sewn around its rim.

Beside these men, beside the few women, two boys came through the Gap into Grover. One came and went; the other stayed.

The first, a short, sturdy boy with a tooth missing in front, and dirty brown hair, was caught late, riding a scrub old horse, a plow horse it had been, most likely, down the hills from the west. He was well onto Spade Bit when Bud Bent saw him and rode him down. Possible the boy intended no harm—possibly never even heard of the Grover fight, or knew that Leslie and Mrs. Dowd were on the place.

His bad luck.

Bent was the oldest of the drovers, chunky, weathered, bearded, tough as an oak stump. He rode the boy down, read him off as a trespasser, knocked him off his plowhorse with a fist the size of a cabbage, and beat him with the bitter end of his lariat.

Bent left the boy weeping, tears and snot commingled on his face, and nothing more was ever seen of that boy on the Bit.

The second boy came to the gate not three days after the dangerous man from Austin, Thompson, had come to call. The boy rode in on a neat little pinto, rode to the gate, and sat, smoking a Bull Durham cigarette.

When he'd been there awhile, Jay Clevenger, who was working a string of mares into the east pasture, saw him, fired a shot to let the others know, and then rode to the gate to see what was up. He had no choice but to leave the mares trailing, and two of them turned back into the north pasture when he was gone.

The boy sat his saddle, smoked, and watched.

Clevenger came up on him—Potts riding down too, kicking his horse up hard so as not to miss any excitement—and saw a young boy and no man. The boy was a hard-bitten seventeen or eighteen maybe, with a leaned-down face, lined like a man's now from weather, or hunger, or both. A lean face, and odd light brown eyes, and nothing much for an outfit. A brown canvas coat cut short, jean trousers and a jean shirt, and a wide-brim leather hat with rawhide stitching up the crown. An old Remington .44, as well, likely a conversion from cap and ball, and looking a sight too big for the boy, was stuck down through his belt. Bare metal, no holster, not even a homemade. He had no rifle. No shotgun, either.

When Clevenger rode up, the boy nodded and swung down from his paint. Clevenger thought he might have done that to ease his ass after a long ride and long wait, or to clear his pistol steadier if he had to. Clevenger had not been a cowpoker all his life.

"No strangers are welcome here, boy. You mount up and be on your way."

The boy stood beside his horse and looked up at Jay, and said nothing in reply.

"You hear me?"

Charlie Potts rode up in a flurry of fresh laid snow. It was a cold, gray day. The snow had quit in the morning, but looked to recommence soon enough.

The boy took a long look at Charlie, who returned the look as strange boys will with each other.

"I hear you have a man shot dead and another arm-broke," the strange kid said. "You'll be needing another hand."

"We don't need you," Charlie Potts said. "Get on

home, little squirt." This although the stranger was taller than Charlie, if not so thick in the shoulders, if a couple of years younger.

The kid paid him no mind, stood looking up at Jay Clevenger, waiting.

"I don't think so," Clevenger said to him. "We need experienced horse-hands."

"How the hell did you find out Sid got shot?" Charlie, pink in the face.

The kid answered Charlie first. "The Doc was talking, in town." Then he looked back at Clevenger. "I've worked with horses all my life—cannon to crouper."

"All your life, huh?" Clevenger smiled at him. "Full sventeen years, I'll bet."

"Eighteen. And I know horses."

"Do you, now?" It was a game Clevenger enjoyed, and he'd caught horse-traders and one halfbreed Comanche with it. "Do you, now?" He pointed down with his thumb at his own mount, a big Roman-nosed article with wide set legs and a sleepy eye. "And how would you call this 'un, kid?"

The boy looked the horse over, squinting. "He's had a splint throwed on his off hind . . ."

"Shit," Charlie said, "any damn fool can see if a horse has throwed a splint!"

"He's got too much belly on him . . . been getting a pint of grain—likely oats—a day the last few days. And that jingle-bob bit don't suit him."

This last nettled Clevenger some, since he'd come to the same conclusion after trying the new bit for two days. "And what *sort* of horse would he be, if you're such a dab at it?"

"Oh, he's a whaler," said the kid, as casual as a

gentleman, "one of those Australian horses or New Zealand, too, I guess."

"You guess . . ." said Jay Clevenger, mighty mortified, who had won more than one bet on his horse's home grass, who had, in fact, won the horse on a bet, with a lumberman who'd had the horse brought in to stake race, lamed it, and put it on a card rather than doctor it out.

"Whoo-eee," cried Charlie, changing sides. Clevenger had stuck him for a dollar on Charlie's wrong call of Morgan and hunter crossed. "You're smarter than you look, kid," he said. "That's sure one up your windpipe, Jay."

The kid looked over at Charlie without smiling, then looked back at Jay Clevenger, who was mighty tempted to boot his smart ass for him and set him on the road smoking.

"*If* you work for us," he said, "you'll be doing chores, not horse-handling and you'll be humping your butt to get 'em done." No use playing the sore-head—not when it would make folks laugh all the more. Now, where in the pure hell had this saddle-bummer boy even seen a whaler?

"Fair enough," the kid said, as if it were a deal.

"Not so fast," Clevenger said. "You got more than me to deal with. You'll talk with Missus Dowd and she'll hire or she won't." He sat his saddle for a moment more, looking the kid over. "Are you honest, or a liar?" Clevenger had found that inquiry to unsettle men, and tell something about them.

"You'd have no way to tell," the boy said, quick as a wink, "whatever answer I gave." And went to his pony and climbed up.

It occurred to Clevenger that this boy had had

schooling. Likely could write as well as read, likely could cipher, too. It made him curious to see how much of the elephant the kid had seen at fifteen or thereabouts.

"You get a job here . . . you better know there's likely to be some trouble."

"Very bad trouble?" the kid said, looking sharp.

"Not too bad any more, huh, Jay?" said Charlie Potts.

"Well," the kid said. "If it's not too bad, I'll stay. But if it *gets* too bad, I'm leaving."

Charlie laughed, but Jay Clevenger was pleased to hear a pup so young show such sense. He turned his horse to lead the kid through the gate. "Come on, then, and see if Missus Dowd'll talk to you."

Charlie fell in beside the boy, and commenced to run his mouth as he was wont to do. "Say," he said, "you hear who we got up here? Stayin' on?"

"I hear you got some old gunman here, shot up."

"What else you hear?"

"Charlie," Clevenger called back over his shoulder, "shut it up." Charlie subsided.

As they rode the half mile up to the house, Clevenger reviewed in his mind the kid's appearance, his way of talking. The dull shine on the bare steel of the old Remington, the dull shine of the pinto's coat. Pistol and pony well curried. He'd know what that might mean in an older man—an older boy, even.

He called back over his shoulder. "What name you using?"

"My own," the boy called back, "Lee Morgan."

"Hell, I use my own, too, and damn proud of it," said Charlie. "I don't know about old Jay . . . say, Jay! You using the McCoy?"

"Lookin' for trouble, are you Charlie?" Clevenger called back.

"No siree! Not with an old smoker like you, I'm not!" Charlie said, and made a funny face when Clevenger turned in his saddle and stared at him. More quietly, to the kid, "Jay's OK. A little mean, that's all." Then rolling back in his saddle as his sorrel took a hummock, "What the heck, I'm sort of mean myself. Not as mean as George, but I guess I'm mean enough to get along."

The kid smiled a little at the funning, but said nothing.

"Can you use that big revolver there you got?"

"I think I can, well enough."

"Shit, not pullin' from your belt, you can't. I'd say you ought to get a holster or leave that weapon in your roll. You got the makins?"

The kid, Morgan, passed over his sack of Bull Durham, and rode easy beside Potts, looking around as he rode, looking over the ranch country.

CHAPTER TWO

THE LAND here was high—even for high mountain country—the first big wide-tabled sweep of the hills up into the real Rockies. Only scant miles to the west, the first great peaks loomed over, their summits white deep into the timber line, even this early in the winter. The only green was the deep, thick green of the pines, running in long streaks across the mountain shoulders, the ridges and hollows of the hills. In the draws, in a creek gully they rode by, the hardwood trees stood bare as bones.

Winter this high would be fierce and windy, the wind carrying the cold down from the peaks above—driving that cold deep into the rider's muscle and gut, spiking him with it, stiffening him, making him feel that if he fell off his mount chasing, he was likely to smash the way a mirror might, when he struck the frozen ground.

The boy was not long past eighteen, but he came from mountain country, almost as high as this, and he knew high mountain cold in a high mountain winter. How it made all tasks more difficult, and some more dangerous.

Hard on the horses, too. Ice cuts . . . ice-balls in

their hoof-frogs. Falls through fooling snow onto stobs and rocks. Slips, and slides on ice. Broken legs . . .

Nothing new to any of that. Of course, this was a bigger place. Bigger horse herd to care for. Other things.

When they rode into the house yard, Clevenger said, "Stay mounted," dismounted himself, and climbed the porch steps to knock. While he waited, Clevenger stepped a little aside, and turned slightly too, so that he had the kid in view. He had not forgotten the well curried Remington, plain belt carry or not. He was pleased to see, when he glanced, that Charlie Potts wasn't entirely wool gathering, either. Truth is, they were both a little touchy remembering how they hadn't stopped that Texican who'd ridden in to break Sid Sefton's arm. They'd let him by, and it had been left to Catherine Dowd to run him off.

Hard to forget something like that . . .

Clevenger and Potts both kept their eyes on young Lee Morgan, when they heard the lady's footsteps coming to the door.

She opened it, and came out onto the porch.

Catherine Dowd had been cooking. Beef soup, and two canned peach pies. She had her white apron on, and her arms were bare and floury to the elbows. She was a very handsome woman, with clear, direct brown eyes, a long, lovely white face, and white arms, as well, even without flour on them. Her rich brown hair was braided, and pinned up in loops of honey brown. She wore no paint on her face, was trim-figured for a big woman, and looked every inch a lady and no nonsense.

"Ma'am," Clevenger said, "boy here is lookin' for

work. Says he knows something about horses . . ."

"Does he, Mister Clevenger?"

"Yes, Ma'am."

"What's your name, young man?" The boy had taken his hat off, showing soft dark blond hair . . . a last sign of his childhood, she thought. Need a haircut, too. God comfort his mother, with a son roaming this country like a dog . . . winter coming and here . . .

"Lee Morgan, Ma'am." Nothing more to say, apparently. Strange eyes . . . almost amber. Boy needs a bath and a good meal. Several good meals.

"You understand that if I hire you, Lee, you will have to work very hard? We're short of a good deal we could use on this ranch. We make up those shortages with perspiration."

Nod. Understood "perspiration," then. That funny Charlie Potts had needed it translated.

"Mister Clevenger says you appear to know horses. We run no fancy stock here. Only solid saddle-breds with good bottom. Work horses for cattlemen. Draft horses for light coaches. But we treat our stock gently, young man. When you rest your horse, and go to cut out one of Spade Bit's to work, remember that. If you run a Spade Bit horse, you had better have a good reason for it. And I will have no rider wear Spanish spurs, or use a punishing bit."

He's listening to me very patiently. A quick look up and down me, more like a man than a boy half-grown. Reminds me of someone—looks like no one I've ever known . . .

The boy sat quiet, waiting for her to go on. Catherine Dowd noticed his hands, large-knuckled, nails broken, chapped and calloused from work. Big hands, a grown man's hands. But his wrists, thin and wiry, were still the wrists of a boy.

"There is something else you should know. We've had some trouble here. I hope it is almost over; perhaps it is over, but we've had trouble." She stepped across the porch to speak up to him directly. "Persons have come up here to the ranch out of . . . curiosity. And perhaps to make trouble. My . . . friend . . . Mister Leslie, was a gunfighter, a fighting man of some note. He lies in the house badly wounded, and . . . not, not likely to recover. I intend that he be spared more trouble . . . from anyone.

"If you stay . . . I will expect that you try . . . try at least, to defend Spade Bit against . . . intrusions. As well as you can."

Jay Clevenger and Charlie Potts felt like two cents at this, but didn't exchange glances. It was too embarrassing to exchange glances over.

"Mister Clevenger and Mister Potts, and our other people, have been very good . . . brave, in helping us."

That helped a bit, not much. But by god they'd like to see the man who'd have stood against the Texican. Let old Leslie wake up and get out of that bed and come and try it! That Texican had put paid to Sid—and damn fast!

"So, if you want to work here—we pay forty dollars and found, and another ten dollars if you'll run your horse in the cavvy."

The boy, job hungry as he was supposed to be, still sat looking down at her like an Englishman, thinking about it.

Who in the world does this boy remind me of . . .?

Then he said, "I'll take the job, Ma'am," and was on the crew.

Buckskin Frank Leslie dreamed a long dream of names . . . of gun flashes in the dark . . . a woman's white breasts, also in night's darkness, lit only by the moon. It was a long, long dream . . . so long, that it ceased being a dream for him, though sometimes, in that dreamed life, he suspected it could not be real.

He met men in that dream, Mexican ranchers . . . sea captains, drovers, lumberjacks and miners. Rich men, too, with fat gold watches, round as their women, tucked into vest pockets.

These men all had questions for him, and he and they lived their dream lives for some time considering those questions. And, if the answers were unpleasing, something fearful happened. Animals were sent after him. Talking horses. Dogs with pistols at their waists. Two cats with small knives to work upon him if he slept within his sleep.

Yet, these imaginings were not always dire. The two cats, for example, became friends of his, and would use their small knives to peel apples when he wanted, although the taste was never right, he being in a dream.

One of the cats, particularly, became a friend of his, and he regretted that animal's loss when the woman woke him, one day, to make him eat.

It took him two weeks to remember Catherine fully—to remember as well the fight that had crippled him. Rather, the shot in the back.

For days after that, he thought it was still summer. Thought so until he glimpsed Catherine, through the half-open bedroom door, carrying a load of wood to the stove. Then he knew it was wood, and not sunshine, that had kept him warm. When he'd asked, then, Catherine had opened the curtains for him, and he'd seen the thin line of snow upon the sill.

A long sleep.

It took more time, more days, before he noticed that his left side, his left hand would disobey him. Disobeying him as he lay down in bed, and would likely disobey him if he tried to stand up . . . to walk. He decided not to try it, afraid of what he might discover.

He did sit up, though. One morning, Catherine refused to give him his breakfast unless he tried to sit up. She put pillows behind him, and helped him, her hand under his odd left arm and, finally, he did sit up, sweating from the effort, his left side prickling from the exertion, as if it were asleep. Then, she gave him his breakfast—a soft boiled egg and a biscuit—and he kept it down.

He didn't recognize the doctor, either, when he came, and pulled down the sheet and blankets, and gently turned him over onto his stomach. When the doctor hurt him, he began to remember him, and said, "God damn it, Nicholson . . ." and, to his surprise, began to cry like a little baby, and went to sleep before the doctor was finished.

Doctor Nicholson, for his part, usually sleepy and slow moving, was considerably agitated when he came out of the bedroom several minutes later.

"By God . . . by God, Mrs. Dowd." He'd stopped being embarrassed by the "Mrs. Dowd" part some months before. "I believe we've done it!" He had to stop and clear his throat. "The paralysis, now . . . I don't know. I don't know about that. Some residual for sure. Some residual. Do you know how unlikely a successful surgery upon the spine . . . ? By God! I don't think a Boston surgeon could have done better!" He noticed that Mrs. Dowd was looking pale, saw her hand, white-knuckled, holding the back of a chair.

"My dear madam," he said to her, "between us, we've saved his life—and after such injuries." He took up her free hand and patted it. "Not entirely out of the woods, though. An infectious gathering . . . a quinsy, pneumonia. Any of these might still kill him. The back wound is still draining."

"Jesus damn that bitch," said Catherine Dowd, and Doctor Nicholson was quiet. The young prostitute, Marcia Porter, who had pulled the trigger on a bulky English pistol aimed at Frank Leslie's back, was now in the Territorial Prison. Would be there, working in the canvas mill, for seven years—and had received that long a sentence, Leslie having no reputation as an angel, only, gossip had it, as a farewell gift of political pressure from Mrs. Dowd's strange little husband to the handsome wife who was betraying him.

An odd enough situation. But, looking at Mrs. Dowd's face now, Nicholson had the impression that Marcia Porter was lucky to be where she was.

"What must we do, now?"

"Keep him warm and quiet. He's still childish, but that will end soon enough, in a few days, and then he'll want to do more than we should let him."

"I'll keep him still."

"Read to him, sit him up when you can. He needs to be taking deep breaths, taking air into his lungs."

"Yes . . . I'll see to it."

Indeed she would, the doctor thought, and reflected on how lucky a man Frank Leslie had proved to be—to take a wound in his back that should have killed him, and, as well, to have this woman so deeply fond she would disgrace herself to be with him, a killer notorious throughout the country.

He also thought that Leslie, alive and improving in health, would prove a renewed target for hoodlums and gunmen intent on polishing their reputations at the expense of a man half-crippled and past his best. He shared neither of these thoughts with Catherine Dowd.

The boy, Morgan, proved out. He did the shit-chores Jay Clevenger handed him without whining or dodging, carried feed buckets and feed sacks out to the corrals, salt chunks out to pasture, mended home fences, and went out in the wagon to cut a cord or two of new posts, freighted them in, dug the post holes, and ran a new line of barbed wire along the tree line above the north pasture.

He seemed not to mind the cold that had the other drovers, Potts, Bent, Clevenger and the others, breathing on frozen hands to limber them for rope work or pitchfork work, come to that.

The boy stayed thin, despite McCorkle's best efforts to feed him up. McCorkle, erstwhile cooky on Broken Iron, had insisted on following Mrs. Dowd off that ranch, even when she ordered all of those employees to stay and work for little Mathew Dowd's manager, Harold Fox. The other men stayed, when some would have preferred to come up to Spade Bit and work her horses—she and Leslie both having been favorites of those men. But McCorkle had refused, and come on to cook up a storm on the Bit, including great meals for the invalid, which Mrs. Dowd intercepted, thanked him for, and disposed of under her green mulch at night, so as not to hurt the cook's feelings.

She also conducted a running contest with him, to the hands' great pleasure, in the matter of pies.

McCorkle bent every effort to fatten the boy, Morgan, and failed. The wiry eighteen-year-old rode and labored and lugged and dug and chored the excess off, three pieces of pie at a sitting, or not. And if he preferred Mrs. Dowd's canned peach to Mister McCorkle's dried apple, Lee Morgan was already smart enough, at his young age, to keep it to himself.

The men liked the boy, too, except George Peach, who didn't care for him, or anyone else. George was a rough—very big and bulky, his black hair cut short as an Irish hooligan's, his eyes a wide, misleading blue. At twenty, he had come to the Bit with a reputation already made, having shot two men to death in Pierce, Wyoming, in a disagreement over the outcome of a dog fight.

His family was as bad as he was—his brothers, older and out of the territory now (to everyone's relief) being reputed barn burners and woman beaters.

But George, though he had bad blood, was not at all shy in a pinch. He was gut game, fairly fast with his pistol, and, more important, was ready with it. He also enjoyed beating men in fist fights, with whatever necessary kicking, gouging, and biting thrown in. Young, very strong, and a hard case.

Peach, young as he was, would have shortly been

stud duck of any other small crew of drovers. But Clevenger and Butt Bent, hard as nails themselves, and older, held him down. Bent had struck him with a branding iron in Peach's second week on the place, and knocked him silly, Peach claiming when he woke that since he couldn't remember it happening, he was under no obligation to call Bent out for it.

Lee Morgan, however, was not older—nor appeared to be hard as nails, and Peach, out of that ceaseless drive for trouble of his kind, began to pick and worry at the new boy.

The kid would take Peach's ragging, and say nothing to it. This made Peach angrier. Still, perhaps because the boy always carried his Remington revolver—still stuck down into his belt rather than in a proper holster—Peach never attempted to put a hand on him.

The winter work wore at them all. And if this winter was not the winter of eight-six, it was not much more pleasant. Well before Christmas, the big snows were blowing in, drifting high at the sides of barns and sheds, heaping white along the tops of fence rails and roof edges. The horses stepped high through the drifts, and stopped, pawing, to try and clear a patch of fall grass, brown and withered.

They lost a fine colt not much more than a mile from the place. Lost it to white wolves come roaming down from the north.

Sid Sefton, his right arm still wrapped and plastered where the Texican's bullet had smashed it, rode out one morning and found the colt's bones and blood scattered as if it had been hit by cannon fire. And the wolf tracks in the snow. The distracted mare, bite wounds at her belly and haunch, wandered nickering in a wide circle around the spot, nuzzling at the bloody spots frozen on the snow.

Sid had unlimbered his Winchester, a new rifle, a pre-Christmas gift, apparently, found by Sid on his bunk one evening after he had come back in from giving young Morgan whatever help he could cutting fence posts and hauling them. Not much help, really, except story telling, and demonstrations of the art of one-handed cigarette rolling.

There the Winchester had been, brand new, successor to the handsome if underpowered Henry, and lying across his old blankets with his name burned into the side of the stock. *Sidney Sefton.* Catherine Dowd had been seen walking to the bunkhouse that afternoon, with a long package wrapped in brown paper.

"Darn well worth a busted arm!" as Sidney said, working hard to learn to manage the piece one-handed, which was possible, but not easy.

Everyone knew it was a gift to Sid in return for that boy's brave foolishness on Mrs. Dowd's porch. George Peach said it was a shame that Sid hadn't got shot through the head; then he might have got a Gatling, and a team to draw it. It was a thorn in George's side that he had been out herding when Ben Thompson came calling all the way from Texas. The others made careful fun of George about that, saying he might have done this or that, but he would have done this or that with wet pants. Peach, who, to give him credit, could take a joke, just grumbled, and said they'd see.

So, the winter came down, and came down hard, and Sefton came riding in a day after he'd found the colt chewed and dead and scattered. He'd doctored the mare, trailed, camped the night, and trailed again, and when he rode back into headquarters, he had two raw wolf-skins rolled and tied across his saddle-bow. His horse, a chunky gray named Pow-wow, and one of the old reliables in Spade Bit's cavvy, was damn displeased by the wolf-hides, and had given Sid a good deal of trouble, riding in. The Busted Wing, as Sid was lately called by his fellows, had had his one hand full, riding, hunting, skinning, and riding again. It had been very cold.

The white wolves hadn't left the hills after that, but they'd ranged further from headquarters, and had taken no more young horses.

The hands had heard that the old gunman at headquarters house looked like to stay alive. Could have told that even without the town gossip when they rode in, two and three together, to drink and play cards—neither of which could be indulged in at the ranch—could have told it by Catherine Dowd's manner. By the look on her face.

"I hear," George had said, "that he can't move not a damn thing but his head. A dead meat cripple, heel to neckbone." It was the sort of talk the men heard in town. The sort of presence they felt on the ranch, too. A happy lady and a quiet, shuttered house, all but one window at the back. The bedroom window.

"Don't hardly see how he can do a full-blooded woman any good at all." Peach again, and got such cold looks from Potts and Sefton that he subsided, mumbling.

Some renewal of interest in Grover, at the doctor's news. Some renewal of interest in Boise and Butte and Elkhorn, as well. Two newspaper men came down through the winter weather, and sat on the

Grover House porch and smoked the house cigars, and ate beefsteak courtesy of their daily expense accounts, figuring, as newspaper men do, to be able to explain the cost as business, later.

These men came down, and poked about, and one rode out to the ranch. The boy, Morgan, rode down to the gate when he saw the winter-rough coat of the livery nag, uncurried, the newspaper man stumbling back and forth in the snow, waiting to be noticed. Both these men had been frightened by town talk about the ferocity of the Spade Bit boys.

The boy, Morgan, had not seemed ferocious to the newspaper man as they talked, had simply said the owner wanted no company. Had then accepted a dollar to ride up to headquarters and ask specific. Said he would do that later, and meantime it would be better for the reporter to ride back to town and wait for his answer.

The reporter, a well set up young man who fancied himself as a skilled boxer, then requested his dollar back.

"No."

Used abusive language.

No reply—or rather the same reply that George Peach had gotten to his ragging. An acknowledging nod. Not a swing out of the saddle to fight in the snow, not even the hint of a move to the vicinity of the butt of the big Remington.

An acknowledging nod. The dollar put away in the back pocket of his jeans.

The well set up reporter climbed back up on his stable plug, hauled his head around, and booted the animal off, observing loudly that the day of the drover as a lord on horseback was near its end—and welcome.

Lee Morgan, wrangler now, since he was working a horse ranch, was not insulted. That evening, he approached the headquarters hourse, for the first time—except for hauling chores—since he'd been hired on, knocked, and asked Mrs. Dowd if she cared to see a reporter from Boise.

She said no.

Next Saturday, on his trip to town, together with Bud Bent and Ray Clevenger, looking like a tired boy with two tough old uncles, Morgan had looked the reporter up, found him at the Grover House front desk with his wicker suitcase, packed and ready, beside his foot, and told him then and there that Mrs. Dowd preferred not to see him.

The reporter, to his credit, had laughed, and given the boy two bits, additional. Then he'd gone out to catch the coach, a kidney buster Corcord with extra-wide iron rims for winter going.

It was the winter, more than anything else, that damped further interest in a wounded gunman recovering from a fight. That, and that the news surrounding the Grover fight had been long out and worn out.

Except for Peach, then, who could never be content until he had put a man in his place—or been put there by him. the Morgan boy found himself well enough liked, if thought occasionally odd.

He never pistol practiced, for one thing—never joined the others back of the corral, when there were no horses down there to be spooked, to waste cartridges they couldn't afford popping away at bean cans and boards, and some, like George Peach and Charley Potts, trying their fast draws.

Lee Morgan sat on the fence for those sessions, and never joined in. He would watch, watch close as a banker counting money. But he never joined in.

"What in the world do you carry that piece for, Sissy Britches?" Peach would say to him, shucking spent rounds from his long-barrel Peacemaker. "You sure don't never shoot the damn thing." And would replace his revolver in its holster, face his bean can, set himself, square his shoulders, shake his right hand a little looser . . . and draw and shoot. A fairly fast draw, in fact, and a good hit to follow it, more often than not. Peach was good with a gun—and of course, and more important, ready.

None of the others were slouches, either, though Bud Bent was slow getting his revolver out. They were each of them better than most with a gun. Certainly better than most drivers or wranglers, whose busted fingers, ripped-off fingernails, arthritis, and lack of cash for cartridges, kept most of them from being really handy with a weapon.

But Catherine Dowd had chosen men unusual in that regard, and the Bit people were canny with guns. Except, possibly, the Morgan boy. And Mrs. Dowd paid them each a box of cartridges a week, .45 or .44 or .44-40, additional to their pay, if they would practice; and they were happy to do that.

She had not offered cartridges to the boy, and he didn't take those offered to him by his fellows. So, for the whole of the long winter, they never saw him shoot.

Then, in the Spring, Charlie Potts saw him, talked about it, and got George Peach killed.

The doctor came out once a week—give him credit, all the more since he loved comfort—came out once a week in every weather through the winter, came out in a sleigh the months of January and March to see Frank Leslie, and watch him slowly, slowly come to life.

Nicholson had not been thought much of a doctor, and no serious surgeon at all. But this case, which everyone knew well to be as close to hopeless as could be—Leslie having already been soundly shot by the monster, Pace, before ever he was given the *coup* by the whore's back shot—had seemed to waken the doctor to a higher order of practice. The man before, who had been indolent, careless, and fat—a doctor, as the trappers might say, *faut de mieux*, had become, since his wonderfully lucky knife work on Leslie's spine, a considerable medical man, determined, and trustworthy. He certainly became more honest, and told people straight out if he felt unable to cut and cure them.

He still drank, but only after church on Sundays, and since this became well known, the people in town and on the surrounding ranches were more careful in those hours.

Every week, the doctor would come out, enter the house, have a piece of pie, receive the week's bulletin of recovery from Mrs. Dowd, and then march with pleasure into the bedroom to find Frank Leslie sitting up in bed (December) and reading or eating a baked apple drenched in milk from the Jersey Mrs. Dowd kept out in her garden shed, and that Lee Morgan had to haul hay to morning and night, blizzard or not. Later in January, Nicholson found his patient, more often than not, fretting in a rocking chair, reading a year-old *Harper's Weekly*. Nicholson, to his additonal credit, augmented that stuff with an occasional *Police Gazette*, and, with Mrs. Dowd out of the room, discussion of what opera dancer or Floradora was suspected of doing what with whom in San Francisco or Saratoga.

Deeper—and darker—news of the Life, the doctor didn't know, and Leslie didn't ask. It was on one of these "rocking chair" visits, that Nicholson let slip—only slightly—some notion of the public attention, and occasional intrusions, that Spade Bit, and Mrs. Dowd, had suffered.

The man before him then, thin, white in the face, looking a weary gray-haired fifty and more, straightened up in his chair, a change coming over his face, and stretched out an arm to take the doctor by the lapel of his suit.

"Who?" the patient asked—not patiently.

It took Nicholson some time to convince Leslie that it had been a general sort of harrassment, not a vendetta by any persons in particular.

He thought he succeeded in calming the man, and perhaps he did, but not altogether. A day later, in the evening, Catherine Dowd found that Leslie had managed to get from his chair to a living room chest—likely by crawling—and taken the Bisley Colt's from it. That night, when Leslie was asleep, she found the revolver hidden behind the headboard of the bed. Oiled, and loaded.

She left it there.

The winter, as it ran, was remarkable only for its weather, and Frank Leslie's recovery. At Christmas, thinking it was time, Catherine had the hands into the house and in combat with McCorkle, fed them and a neighbor rancher named Pawley and his huge wife almost to death around a trestle table of live oak planks. There was whiskey for Leslie and the Pawleys, beer—from the Black Ace in town—for the hands. Two hams, beefsteaks, fried chicken, sweet and white potatoes, pickled beets and beans, stewed onions, hot gingerbread, hot cornbread, a loaf of fine white bread, and a sourkraut salad. Peach pies and McCorkle's apple pies to finish, with vanilla iced-cream—a bucket full of that.

It was the first time any of the hands had seen Leslie close up and for a while since the shooting. Bent and Sid Sefton had known him to talk to before that, when he was regulator for Mathew Dowd's Broken Iron.

Leslie now, looking frail, sat in his rocking chair at the head of the table, Catherine Dowd beside him, for the whole of the Christmas meal. He was wearing dark gray wool pants, and a white silk shirt. Mrs. Dowd had taken these in to fit his gauntness, but the clothes still hung on him in folds. All the people at the table glanced at him from time to time as they ate, watching the thin-skinned beaky face, scar-sliced down the left cheek, veiled dark gray eyes, his hands, handsome as a gent's, as he toyed with a piece of buttered bread. He looked all done in.

"A miracle just to see the poor man sitting up instead of flat in a box in the dirt." Mrs. Pawley to Nate Pawley on their way home. No easy way, even by moonlight, in a sled runner buckboard pulled by a two-horse team. Mister Pawley had no interesting reply, and kept an habitual silence. It was a still, cold night; the distant mountains, the hills at their skirts, the pines along the trail, all seemed set at the same distance, perfectly clear on a field of white. Still, and cold. "A miracle," said Mrs. Pawley, as if Mister Pawley had disagreed.

"Be better off dead," Charlie Potts said, "than sit around lookin' like a body corpse breathin'." He and the other Spade Bit hands discussed the supper in the bunkhouse after. The next day would be easy—mending harness, carpentry, doing some doctoring, setting up a new forge for Bent to shoe at. Getting in firewood for the house and the bunkhouse. Hauling out hay for the roaming stock. Forking it down for the horses corraled and stabled. Breaking ice in the tanks and troughs and carrying some of the penned horses. Whitewashing the colt barn . . . might do some field-rat hunting after doing that, if Chunker—the ranch's sorry hound-fice—could be persuaded to come to scratch.

"Better off dead," Charlie Potts said, "than be like that." Clevenger and Peach agreed. Bent said the man was getting better. "See him use that left hand? Them fingers bend and everything. You wait for Spring. I say that sport will have a revolver on again." Laughter. "That fellow's a dead letter," Charlie Potts said, to nods. "He ever lifts a pistol again, it'll be to pick his teeth with the sight."

Lee Morgan, wearing, like the others, his best shirt, his best trousers, his long, soft brown hair still slicked down with Macasser oil, sat on the edge of his bunk, and said nothing. Listened.

He had said little during the supper. "Thank you and no thank you," to passings of the butter, the jam, (blueberry jam Mrs. Dowd had cooked down in summer, wild strawberry jam McCorkle had cooked down when he heard about the blueberry jam) and a request for more fried chicken when the platter seemed stuck at the other end of the table.

Mrs. Dowd noticed that the boy had filled out at least a little in the months at the Bit—more muscle than food-fat, she thought. He still stood in need of a haircut, didn't seem to have had more than one, and that likely a rough bunkhouse shearing, since he'd come on the place. She noticed the boy taking his share of looking up the table at Leslie. More than his share, maybe. Looking, she thought, to see the holder of a famous name—unlikely, she thought, to draw a lesson from Frank Leslie's current state. Sick, old before his time, half-crippled. Quiet.

After the pie and ice cream, Mrs. Dowd had invited everyone into the parlor—the first time, for most of the hands—and sat at the small spinet, and played Christmas songs, including some pretty German ones that no one had heard before. "*Stille Nacht*," she called one. She played *Good King Wenceslaus*, too, and everybody sang that one. George Peach had a nice tenor, and sang out like a Trojan—he and Mrs. Pawley vying to see who could sing loudest.

There had been a bit of a tight right after supper, when folks were going out to the necessary—tramping out the kitchen door and through fifty feet of two feet of snow—or filing into the parlor. For when folks started up from the table—some of them so full they had to try more than once to stand—Frank Leslie got up, too. At first, Catherine Dowd had gotten up and gone to his side to help him, but he'd put her hand aside with his limp left, placed his right hand flat on the table top, set his jaw, and slowly,

slowly risen to his feet. People at the table and getting up from it had stared—until he sent a glance like a gunshot down the trestle planks. Then they looked down at their plates, except for the boy, Morgan.

Leslie had gotten to his feet, steadied himself a moment more with the edge of the table, then turned and taken two staggering strides to the kitchen wall, rested on it, and leaning on the wall like the shoulder of a friend, slowly worked his way out of the kitchen, to a straight back chair inside the parlor doorway.

And there he'd sat the rest of the evening, with a cup of coffee held on his lap. And when Mrs. Pawley asked if he wouldn't care to sing in with them, from over there, if he pleased, replied that he wouldn't dare match his poor voice with an angel's trumpet like her own. Which left her in some puzzlement whether she should be pleased.

Afterward, young Lee listened to the hands discuss their supper and the damaged gunman, and said nothing of either, except that the chicken had been prime.

Up at the house, when she had pumped a tub full of water, added hot water to it from the stove, and put the dishes and pans in to soak, Catherine Dowd had gone into the bedroom to find Frank Leslie lying on the bed in his nightshirt, watching the doorway, waiting for her.

"You need that Indian woman of yours, Catherine; householding, and looking after me is too damn much!" Catherine Dowd had brought no servant with her to Spade Bit. No elegant clothes or fixings, either.

"No," she said to him, "it isn't." And went and sat at her small dresser, and commenced to un-pin her hair. It gave Leslie great pleasure to watch her do that, and she knew it. "I like to do for you, my dear," she said, tugging the small hairpins loose, one by one, so that slowly her rich hair, smooth and shining as Mexican chocolate, fell below her shoulders in cascades.

"Too damn much and too damn long," he said, sat half up and shook his numb left hand as if to wake it. He tried to clench the hand, and slowly, it did make a weak fist. Catherine got up from her dresser, her hair falling down her back like a girl's, came over to him, and sat down on the side of the bed.

"Frank," she said. "Do you know what it means to me to have you back from the dead? To hear you speak . . . to watch you while you sleep?" She put her strong small hand on his weak large one. "I'm happier now than I have ever been. So don't you feel sorry for me—or yourself, either."

"If you're saying that I'm a fool for luck—weak side, or not—I know that." He lay back down, and she got up from the bed and went to her wardrobe to undress herself. She turned to face him as she did, so that he could see her better.

CHAPTER THREE

SPRING CAME slowly to the high country.

Late in March, the drifts, still ridged and laced with ice patches, leaned high against the building walls in Grover, still mixed with frozen mud in Grover's streets. Up on the range, past Broken Iron and on up to the Bit, the drifts were deeper, the winds colder, the pines still sometimes breaking with reports like pistol shots in the pale, sunny afternoons.

The snow, ice-surfaced from slight thaws and freezing, creaked like a weak roof if a wrangler walked across it—broke and fell right in under a horse's hoof. Tough going, and tough working. The stock went limping with cut pasterns and fetlocks, sliced on rough ice edges among the snow as they grazed thrown hay, pawed for year-old grass. Even the stallions were subdued. Ace muttered in his double stall, barely trying to arch his head over the door to bite the passersby. The vision of the great gray head, a rolling eye, yellow tombstone teeth, and a hard and empty "clack," as the stallion missed even the passer's hat. Tosspot was loose with the mares—had been all winter—and seemed tired of the cold. Any man who cared to could go up to him afoot, lift his foot, hook out the frogs, do anything they liked.

The stock, and the hands, were weary of winter.

Different appearances up at the house. There, the long winter, still and bitter cold, white and sound-muffled even with an occasional hissing wind, had seemed to plant new heat, new strength into Catherine Dowd—who, when she came out of the house one icy, bright late March morning, came out onto the porch as rosy, as full and smooth as a young farm girl, and smiling. It seemed, or might have if someone had been watching, that she towed from that day the whole Spring behind her, and brought it out of her small house. As she brought the damaged killer out a few days later, holding him by his left hand.

Buckskin Frank Leslie looked no younger for his winter's peace. But stronger. He walked like a man again, not like a stumbling child. He held a strong stick in his right hand, and with that, he walked like a man. They still held hands, her small strong one to his large weak left hand—but like lovers. Leslie, on the day he came out walking with Mrs. Dowd, was smoking a cigar.

He walked out into the snow—and trudged through it, puffing a little at the effort—to the bunkhouse. George Peach was there, and Bud Bent, both mending leathers. They heard odd footsteps on the threshold, heard Leslie saying something to Mrs. Dowd, and there he was. He stood in the doorway, looking at them, looking down the length of the bunkhouse, as if he'd never seen a wrangler, nor where he lived.

"Morning, boys."

"Morning, Mister Leslie," said Bent.

George just stared. "Sure glad to see you up and around," Bent added.

"Haven't been doing my share of chores, for sure," Leslie said, looking down at them, leaning on his stick. "I don't mean to interrupt your work, either—just came out on a stretch-my-legs."

"Morning," said George.

"You'd be George Peach," Leslie said, looking at him. "I recall your singing at the party . . ." He smiled in a pleasant way. "I fear I was a flat at that Christmas party."

The wranglers said oh, no, he'd done fine.

"Well, I'll be doing better soon. Better enough to do some choring." He turned in the doorway to go, then stopped and looked back at them. "You let the other boys know, will you? That I am personally obliged to them for their service to Mrs. Dowd. I thank you all for doing that."

No need for that, Bud and George Peach said. No need for that at all.

When he was gone, Bud Bent turned to George and said, "Well, well."

"Pretty lively, for a body-corpse," George said.

Most days, after that, Leslie came outside. Even in the rain when the snow turned wet and wetter well into April as the weather warmed. He would walk out, the strong stick held in his left hand, more often than not, and limp around the place, not riding, walking. On rainy days, the rain would splash and spatter off his Stetson brim, the shoulders of his yellow slicker, and he would stride around the yard and on out to the corrals, as well. On those days, McCorkle, permanent in the cook shack out beside the bunkhouse, would look out his doorway and see the gunman, limping, scarred, no longer young or nearly young, digging his walking stick into the puddled mud at every step, his dark gray Stetson tugged down low. And across the corral, across the yard, past the porch, McCorkle saw on these occasions the curtained form of Mrs. Dowd as she stood half-concealed, watching Frank Leslie walking through the rain.

McCorkle watched the man and woman both. The boy, Lee Morgan, watched only the man. McCorkle saw that, too.

Morgan, a hard worker and no complaint against him by either Jay Clevenger or Bent, who shared the foremanship as much as one was needed on such a small spread—no more than ten thousand acres, paid for—was more and more at headquarters. Would work harder, faster, it seemed, the sooner to get back to headquarters. And chafed, if kept away. When he was there, at some work or other—digging a cess pit for one—he seemed content, and would work, and watch.

When Leslie came out, which he did most every day as the Spring came fully down—the snow slowly climbing back up into the hills, and then, after pausing a week or two, up further, and further yet, into the mountains—the boy would be on the place, sure as shooting. Watching him. After McCorkle, Jay Clevenger noticed it, but said nothing. At first, he had thought it might be Catherine Dowd the boy was anxious to be seeing, to be near. Natural enough in a boy that age. Wasn't a hand on the place hadn't felt the same some time or other. But soon enough, Clevenger saw that it was Leslie the boy looked at, watched on his walks.

Well, that was natural enough, too, in a young boy. Leslie might be shot to bits, but his was still a great name among fighting men. Plenty of boys Lee Morgan's age would be glad enough for just a sight of Buckskin Frank Leslie, tattered or not.

This impression was confirmed for Clevenger when the Morgan boy, in a bull session one evening at foaling camp—early that year, since Catherine Dowd was determined to lose no baby horses—at the campfire while the hands were japing and yarning, had asked Clevenger if he thought Leslie might soon put on his revolver. It was an odd question, because Lee Morgan asked few of them, and then only about work. Perhaps he thought it made him look childish to be always asking questions. But he asked that one.

"Hell's bells, I don't know, boy," Clevenger said. "Likely never." He pulled a twig out of the fire to relight a pipe gone out, and puffed it glowing. "Man's probably had about all the bang-bang he wants."

"All he's good for," Peach said. "That's for sure." And there was a general discussion of violence and the weariness and common sense that might grow out of it. Even George and Charlie Potts became philosophical. Sid Sefton said it wasn't so. Look at him! and wiggled a healed and useful arm. Gun fought with Ben Thompson—who had scared the liver out of Shanghai Pierce and others at their own banquet in Texas—damn near exchanged shots with the fellow (revolver caught on the holster leather, worse luck) and came out not too bad. Who else here was qualified to talk about it?

"Oh, stuff it!" George said. "That Texican could

have shot you up and down your buttons! and we all know it."

"So you say," Sid said, but didn't push it. George had fallen in love with a whore, Mary Spots—so called from her freckles—who worked in a crib out back of the Black Ace, and this had made him touchy. Mary, who was a nice, sunny girl, though painfully thin and probably a lunger, had put George off in the nicest way, and wouldn't screw him, for fear of making him even more unhappy.

Knowing how troublesome this sort of a thing could be, feelings let loose—and especially feelings in a bulky young brute mighty sudden with his pistol—the men were circumspect in dealing with George.

"So you say," Sid said. "I didn't say I was faster than him."

"I guess not," George said, snorting a fair imitation of Tosspot, lately, who had renewed his interest in the mares. It was getting to be stallion weather, in fact, and Ace—still stalled—had bitten out a chunk of McCorkle's hair when the cook had taken too short a cut past his stall the week before.

"I guess not," George said again, snorting, and got up from the fire, loosed a farewell beany fart, and went to his soogins, rolled up in them, and went to sleep.

There were glances of relief around the fire, except for the kid, Morgan, who never joined in those kinds of exchanged glances—of relief at this or that, of weariness, of resentment at painful orders for difficult work. "You don't think he'll wear his pistol again?" he said, still addressing Clevenger.

"Now why in hell should he? The man's fightin' days are done, boy." And the others agreed.

"His right hand's all right."

"That's so," Bent said, getting up to go to sleep, "but we're not talking about a man's hand."

The boy wouldn't let it alone. Couldn't seem to let it alone. "You're saying that he's lost his nerve, won't take up a fight?"

Clevenger said, "What we're *sayin'* is that the man has *learned* somethin', boy. An' what he learned is, that shootin don't pay."

Still, as the spring seized the country and enriched it with sun and green, pulling, as April ended, the first of the foals out of Spade Bit's mares, young Morgan would be seen watching Frank Leslie now and then, as Leslie strolled—still not riding, apparently wanting the exercise—up and down and around the place. Walking out, now, clear to the pastures. Walking, as Charley Potts said, as much as a Scotchman, limping along, but limping less, swinging his stick as much as he leaned on it.

Sometimes, seeing the Morgan boy nearby at his chores, Leslie would call a greeting to him, lift his stick in a howdy. The man was getting well, no question. Still limped on his left leg, still took care what he held with his left hand. But for the rest, better and better. The Spring, the sun, the high country air seemed to be pouring life back into him. But not youth.

People who came by the ranch, neighbors, now, not sight-curious strangers, would see that Frank Leslie was getting along fine—seen by doctor Nicholson less and less often—and was also no young man. More than middle-aged, in fact, in his face, lined and weathered and scarred as it was.

Younger, perhaps, in his eyes. The same dark gray, the same thrusting look . . . direct from him to you, that they'd had before Pace had come up from Texas, as terrible, as Reverend Shaw had said, as an army with banners, and met his better over pistols at the Grover House.

Mister Leslie's eyes were still young enough to push a man back a little, to straighten him up, at any event. So, the neighbors came by to see him walking, and some people came visiting out of town. Pabst and his new wife, Rex Milford that kept the other feed store. The new marshal, Meagher, came out with some news from Boise. Catherine Dowd had lawyers up there contending with possible trouble over the previous marshal's death, contending successfully, it appeared.

No one came, all Spring, to trouble them. They got fourteen fine colt foals out of their herd. Nineteen fillies. And every one of them lived to get up and run. Two mares were lost—one to some sort of poison weed (Mister Pawley had never seen such symptoms before) and the other to a birthing sickness when she failed to throw the afterbirth completely. Both good horses, each a serious loss. But the herd, in balance, did better than most, and proved a pleasure and a profit from the winter.

In the second week in April, Charlie Potts rode up into the hills to drive some yearlings in, and heard gunfire.

Broken ground, steep ground, lay to Charlie's right, about two hundred yards away. The shooting was coming from there. Charlie was no shy boy; he hauled out his Henry—which had seen better days—and rode to the sound.

There were trees, box alder, bordering those breaks, and Charlie pulled his horse down to a walk and threaded his way through, hearing the regular *slam . . . slam . . .* as he rode. He cocked the Henry, having a sudden vision of some sheep herders killing the Bit stock, shooting the horses down in the broken ground.

He got to a gully's edge, eased his mount past a leaning tree, looked down, and saw Lee Morgan at pistol practice.

It made Charlie pissy mad—to be thrown scared and cautious by a fool wrangler doing shooting when he was supposed, as Morgan was supposed, to be riding circuit fence six miles away. And mending fence, too. Charlie started to spur on down there, and tell that squirt a thing or three—and damn loud.

But he didn't.

He stayed watching.

The Morgan boy was standing, hip-shot, thirty or forty feet away from a winter-split stump. Drawing on that object, replacing his Remington revolver in his wide belt, and drawing and shooting again. He was doing that as regular as a pendulum clock, and all of it easy to see from where Potts watched, perhaps a hundred yards up and to the side. All of it easy to see—except the draw. That was too quick to make out anything but some sudden snapping motion that appeared to come together with the shot.

It was by all odds the quickest pistol-draw that Charlie Potts had ever seen—and he had seen Bassett draw on a man in Fort Smith, and kill him.

This, what the Morgan boy was doing, was something else altogether.

Charlie sat his pony for half an hour there above

the break, and didn't call down to the kid, or wave, or do anything to catch his attention. He watched.

Morgan was not only drawing that piece slick as a whistle—and just from his belt, too, no greased holster, no tricky little steel plate or loop of leather. Just from his belt—the revolver stuck down there as common as dirt. He was only drawing the piece faster than Charlie had ever seen it done.

He was shooting the pure shit out of that stump. Knocking a chunk or splinter loose with every round, as far as Charlie could see. Shooting that stump to pieces at thirty, forty feet. And that out of a draw quick as a snake's strike.

Charlie watched for a little longer, then, carefully, quietly, he backed his pony in behind that leaning tree, and further back, slowly, into the brush. Then he turned him, and rode out of there at a slow walk. Rode until he was well clear of the break, then kicked his pony into a lope, heading up toward the north pastures, and the yearlings.

Charlie reflected as he rode why he'd been so cautious, so quiet and ready to stay unseen. Damned if he knew, really. He and the boy got on well enough, were friendly as was usual in young hands working the same spread. Had nothing against the boy—the boy had nothing against him. But he hadn't called out to him. Hadn't whistled and called out, "Jeeesus Christ-on-a-crutch! Kid! That *is* shootin'!"

No siree. He had done no such thing. And as he rode and thought about it some more, Potts decided why. He had been plain scared; that was why. Lee Morgan had been *too* damn good. And him only eighteen or so. Jesus! Too damn good. And it was why he'd never target-shot with the rest of the boys.

Because they'd see the draw. See that shooting. Too damn good.

For a moment, Charlie wondered if the Morgan boy could be Billy the Kid . . . then decided not. That fellow was buck-toothed, from all accounts, and years older to boot.

No, sir. Lee Morgan was Lee Morgan, and it looked to be more than enough. Charlie remembered the times he, or another of the hands, Sefton, or George Peach, had ragged the boy, set to him to chores and errands, threatened to whip his butt, joking. Charlie felt some relief, now, those matters had not gone further. Had not got to fighting.

God help somebody if they had, he thought. If they'd got to gun-fighting. As for calling down the kid, congratulating him on such fine shooting. Something had kept him from it. Would keep his mouth shut about what he'd seen, too . . .

Something.

And so, he saved his life. Would have saved George Peach's too, if, two weeks later, he hadn't been drunk enough to say just a little.

Sid Sefton and Bud Bent stayed home Saturday. They'd both gone into Grover on Friday afternoon, and were allowed to stay 'till dark, having done Bit's business—the purchase of fencing, Glidden's best. They'd dropped by the Ace, and taken a drink, sat in some faro (and lost to the saloon sharper, Shattuck, some six dollars) and had some jokes with the girls, Brenda and Rose. Mary Spots was asleep, and had been sick.

So, they'd had their towning for the week, and stayed on the place Saturday night, smoking and playing checkers in the bunkhouse with Frank Leslie and McCorkle, who didn't care for town. Leslie won the first match, with young Sidney using his weak left hand to make his moves for exercise, he said. Sid used his recently broken arm for the same, for luck, in vain. Leslie often came by the bunkhouse in the evenings, now, walking much easier, though still with a stick, and the hands liked the visits well enough. Liked it, as well, that Leslie had taken on the chore of feeding the stabled horses, hauling grain and hay bunches morning and night, using his left hand as much as he could.

Mrs. Dowd had tried to persuade him against this, saying it was too soon, would do him harm. But he smiled, and paid her no mind.

While Leslie, then, Bent, Sefton, and McCorkle—who supported the checkers match with cold sliced pork sandwiches and pickled tomatoes—stayed on the place, and could hear, faintly, the music of Catherine Dowd's spinet as she practiced, the other men went in to town.

They rode in with the sunset, just finished with chores, fresh shaved and washtub scrubbed. Clean clothes on every one, and boots greasy with wax polish. They all rode Bit horses, fresh out of the cavvy, even the kid, Morgan, riding a Bit horse named Fandango, instead of his own neat pinto. They were armed, but no more than usual.

Jay Clevenger, George Peach, Charlie Potts, and Lee Morgan.

They rode into town just before dark, left their horses at the rail in front of Banning's, went in, and had a warm-up drink. John Chook, Meagher's deputy, came into Banning's, spoke to them, and had a beer with Clevenger; telling him by the way, of the latest news of Pabst and his girl-bride. The lady had decided to sing a song concert up at the Grover House, and was requiring Elbert Pabst to pay for a small orchestra down from Boise to accompany her.

When this news was passed along, George commenced a singing concert of his own, in imitation of the lady, singing out in a considerable voice, *The Last Rose of Summer.* The others, young Morgan included, joining in, and making such noise that Chook, a small bony man in his thirties—and supposed to be a fighter—shook his head, put his fingers in his ears, and left.

They stayed at Bannings for another two hours, with George impatient to get over to the Black Ace to see Mary Spots. He complained, and bullied and worried at the others until they agreed to go and buck Shattuck's tiger, and see the ladies.

More than half-drunk on beer and rye whiskey mixed, the four of them, with two Broken Iron drovers, Houlihan and Edward Cherry, walked down the boardwalk, down the steep steps, and across a rain muddied Main Street to Ace. They sang all the way. *I Don't Want to Play in Your Yard* and *Step Up, You Ladies!* A man yelled at them from a window down the block, wanting them to shut up—but without effect.

They arrived at the Black Ace in good spirits, bucked and crowded their way through the swinging doors, found the Bit's habitual table besat by four drummers in bright wool suits and punched and kicked those people out in jig time. Then they ordered a pitcher of beer, set-ups of Pennsylvania whiskey all round and hooted the waiter-bartender when he asked if they wanted house beefsteaks. McCorkle didn't leave much appetite running loose in Spade Bit's. The Broken Iron boys sitting with them were out of luck, since they would have had their beefsteaks spit into or soaked with beer if they'd tried to eat them at that table.

Shattuck was off-duty for the while, and the second bartender, Bergstrom, stood in for him at faro and lost the house sixteen dollars to Charlie Potts, who, acting like a sport, stood the next round for the house.

Barrelhouse Brenda came in from the back then, and Mary Spots was with her, looking pale, and thinner than ever.

Right away, George Peach got up like a gentleman, and asked Mary to dance but she shook her head, not feeling "up to bein' stomped on, George," and he made Houlihan, of the Iron, get up from his chair and give it to Mary so she could sit with them. Jay Clevenger asked Brenda to dance, and she said, "You bet!" and hauled him out onto the sawdusted floor and commenced jigging up a storm with him to the music of the player piano, and Doc Flint's banjo. Jay, some fifty pounds lighter, was doing no leading at all, and after getting spun about for a number of measures, commenced to call out for help, which made the patrons laugh.

At this time, George Peach was taken with a need for the necessary, and got up and went out back. The kid, Morgan, who had drunk a good deal more than his usual for some reason, talked across the table to Mary Spots, and asked "How about it?"

Now, Mary had been with several of the boys—certainly with Charlie Potts, and Clevenger and

Edward Cherry of the Iron. But neither she, nor any of the other girls, had been with the kid, though they'd teased him, and promised to "show it to him." He was a handsome boy, though, and they'd talked and giggled about him a bit.

At first, though, not feeling well—and perhaps worried that George might take it hard should he come back and find her gone with another customer—Mary shook her head no and she and the boy were ragged and egged-on by the others, for the fun of it, and perhaps with the object of putting George Peach's nose out of joint. The other people kept this up, and Morgan took a ten dollar gold piece out of his shirt pocket, and gave it to her. So, Mary sighed and stood up, and gave him the thumb to come on.

Mary led the boy out back—expecting at any minute to meet George coming back inside from the privy, and find herself with a fight on her hands and the bartenders to call for help. George was a hard case. She hustled the boy down the back of the Ace and into her crib pretty quick, in consequence.

This was not, in fact, Lee Morgan's first time with a woman. A farm girl from across the mountain valley where his mother had ranched had taught him what was what when he was sixteen.

Mary Spots was, however, his first whore and his first woman in nearly a year. He felt something shy standing just inside the door of the crib—a long closet, rather than a room (eight feet by five), the weeping slat walls plastered with rotogravure pictures from the Boise and Chicago papers brought through by drummers. Flowers. Little children. Society ladies from New York and San Francisco in their fine gowns and furs—that sort of thing. And a chipped enamel basin, a scrap of curled yellow soap, and a towel the kid could see through.

Mary sat down on the cot, pulled her camisole vest up over her head, unfastened her band, and exposed her small, freckled long-nippled breasts to him.

"I don't know if these are a ten dollar pair," she said, "but you can come give 'em a feel . . ."

The boy went over to her, reached down, and began to stroke her, gently, with the tips of his fingers. While he did that, Mary twisted half around, unfastened the side of her short skirt, stood up to lean against him for a moment and let the skirt fall to the dirt floor. "I'm givin' you a good look, kid," she said. "I don't usually peel off, not for ten, not for nothin'."

She sat back down on the cot, naked except for her shoes, then rolled back onto the sheet, brought her knees up, and spread her thin legs. She had as little hair there as a child, ginger-colored, soft and sparse, but her split was violent red, swollen, deep, and raw. She reached down thin dirty fingers to spread it, open it farther. "That give you a stand?" she said, looking up at him through her separated knees. "You can see everything I got—right up inside . . ."

She saw a bulging place at the fly of his trousers. "Now," she said, "now I see somethin'," and sat up to unbutton his pants. Then she slid her hand in and down under the waistband of his underdrawers. "Oh, that's nice," she said, and finished unbuttoning him and pushed his trousers and drawers down to his knees. Lee took the Remington in his hand as she loosened his belt, reached out, and put it down beside the enameled basin.

"Say now, that's a nice whang you got, kid . . . oh,

my . . . that's a nice one." She gripped him with both hands, squeezing him, massaging his cock. She bent closer to see if any pus was coming from the tip, then put her mouth to him and kissed it. "Tastes fine, too," she said, and put her mouth to it again and began to suck on it strongly, moving her head back and forth. She took her mouth away with a wet sound, and looked up at him. "Never had a Frenching, did you? Never had a girl take it in her mouth?" She bent down and kissed it again. "You sure got a sweet one," she said. "I love the taste of this one." And put it into her mouth and began to suck and lick at it, rolling her eyes up to watch him watching her. The kerosene lamp threw hard shadows across her face, the moving bulge in the side of her cheek. Her mouth full of him, Mary Spots breathed heavily through her nose, snorting a little as her head moved back and forth.

Then she let him go, and sat back on the cot, her mouth open, catching her breath. "This is what you men pay for," she said, panting. "A decent woman won't do what we do." She reached out and took his hand. "My, my," she said, "you're shaking all over, aren't you? Truly you didn't have nobody do you like that?" Lee shook his head, and Mary laughed. "Well —now you know what men pay us for." She stroked his cock, absently, looking up at him. "You know what else we do? Do you?"

Lee had to clear his throat. "I guess so."

"You're pretty," she said, and leaned forward on the cot to kiss his thigh. "I'm surprised no sissy tried for you. You're so nice. How old are you?"

"Eighteen."

"Well, you are a handsome boy," she said, and

rested her face against his stomach and kissed him. "Do you know I'm sick?" she said. "I have the consumption."

"I'm sorry."

"I bet."

"No, I am sorry."

"Well," she said. "Everybody goes, sometime. You don't believe it, but it'll happen to you, too. Kids don't believe that, and I know that for a fact, because I didn't believe it either, when I was a kid."

"No, I know it," Lee said. He was starting to feel embarrassed with his trousers down to his knees.

"Maybe," she said. "Maybe you do." She bent forward and sucked at him for a few moments, then leaned back. Her chin was wet with spit. "I'm going to do something for you," she said. "Something you'll always remember—even after I'm dead. Even after years."

She took him by the hips, gripping him with her thin, strong hands, and turned him half-around, shuffling, bound by his lowered trousers, then all the way around. "Bend over," she said. "Don't be scared of me."

Lee hesitated, then bent over, feeling like a fool—that she was going to laugh and spank him like a kid. She didn't do anything for a moment or two, then he felt her pull his buttock cheeks apart, and then felt her mouth on him, the small wet stirring of her tongue, licking, kissing. The warm pressure of her face, pushing against him. The movement of her tongue.

She let him go after a minute or so. He felt the chill of cool air beneath him, the wet between his buttocks. "There," she said as he straightened up, his cock standing out hard as a hickory billet, and hitched awkwardly back around. He was too embarrassed to look down at her.

"There," she said. "That's something your own mother would never do. No decent woman. Now, you won't ever forget me—for doing that to you. You'll always remember Mary Connors, even when I'm dead."

He stood looking past her, at the crib wall, embarrassed.

"You look at me," she said. "I licked your asshole for you, you little son-of-a-bitch, for just a dirty ten dollars! Do you think I do that for ten dollars?"

"I'd remember you, anyway," Lee said. "Without you doing that."

"So you say." She had tears in her eyes. "I've heard that sort of shit before, bucko." She reached out and began to gently rub his cock, gripping it lightly in her hand, stroking up and down. "Feels better than when you do it, don't it?" She took her hand away, bent her head to lick her palm, then gripped him again—her hand sliding on his cock faster and faster.

Lee put his hand on her thin, naked shoulder to steady himself as she worked at him. "I'm doin' this," she said, breathless with effort as her arm pumped, "to save you some burnin' piss."

Lee moaned, sounding like a dreaming child, shook in her hands, leaned over her, and began shooting his jissom over her wrist, spurting it gleaming in lamplight down her arm, in warm drops on the bed. Her thin hand still moved on him, slippery now, milking it out of him as he trembled against her. "Ohhh, yes, now," said Mary Spots. "That's a pretty thing for you to do, isn't it—get your stuff all over a girl . . . Oh, there now, you give it to your Mary. There, now—that's better. Isn't that nicer than the claps, now? Which is what you'd get from my cunny, sweet boy." She squeezed at him gently a time or two more. Squeezing, a last pearl of liquid to the tip of his cock. Put out her tongue, and licked that off.

"There, by God," she said. "You damn well got your ten bucks' worth—didn't you?"

"Yes," Lee said, his hands shaking as he pulled his trousers up while she sat on the cot watching him. It took him a while to get his flies buttoned, to buckle his belt. She sat naked, watching him.

"Don't you think for a minute I do that for everybody," she said. "Don't you think that for a minute."

"No, I don't think so," Lee said, and reached over beside the basin to pick up the big Remington, and slide it down into his belt.

"You better not. You talk about that, and I'll call you a queer in front of everybody. I'll say you're a sissy."

"I won't say anything to anybody."

She got up, bent to pick up her skirt, and put it on, buttoning it at the side. "I know you won't," she said. "You're a nice kid, and wouldn't say anything to hurt a girl who's got the consumption."

"No, I wouldn't."

"Sure to die of it." She wrapped her breast band, and pulled the camisole top on over it. She looked at Lee—standing, she was almost as tall as he, a tall, bone-thin girl—and he saw she was crying. "I'm not that drunk," she said, "that I would put my mouth on a fellow's behind like that." She picked up the threadbare towel and wiped her arm and wrist with it. "But you'll damn sure remember Mary Connors when she's gone!"

"I'll always remember you, Mary."

"You're a god-damned liar," she said, wiped the tears from her eyes with the towel, and tossed it on the bed. "You sure had a lot of that spunk in you. Near to poppin' with it, you were."

George Peach had come into the Ace from the privy just after Mary had gone out with Lee Morgan, had come to the table, and seen she was gone.

"Where'd Mary go?" he said.

"Took a breath of air," Clevenger said.

"A young breath," Houlihan said, who was standing against the wall by the table with his beer in his hand. He hadn't liked Peach making him get up and give his chair to a common split-tail.

"What?"

"Drink your beer, George," Clevenger said. "Cause we're orderin' fresh. Drink up."

George drank his beer down, and put the glass on the table harder than he needed to. "Where's the kid?"

"Takin' a breath of air," Houlihan said.

"You shut up, Tommy." Ed Cherry, who saw some trouble maybe coming, saw no reason for Iron to mix in it.

"What in fuck are you—?" George heaved around in his chair to look up at Houlihan. "What did you say to me?"

"Nothin'—to you."

"Tommy don't mean nothin', George," Cherry said to him.

"Whiskey all 'round?" Charlie Potts had gotten the high sign from Jay Clevenger.

"He better not," George said. "I'll have a whiskey." He reached out and toyed with the glass in front of him. "He better not mean anything."

Charlie stood half-up, and waved Bergstrom over. "Say—" he called out to him. "That Pennsylvania gut. Let's have it round again!" Bergstrom heard him through the noise of some Short-C punchers across the room playing seven-up, and nodded that he got the order.

"Mary went out with that kid?" George said.

"Yeah," Clevenger said, and laughed. "She took him for a yellow ten, too. I guess she felt sorry for him." He glanced at George. "She's a darb, Mary."

"She's the best," George said—and then saw Charlie rolling his eyes across the table at Ed Cherry, making fun.

"God damn you, Charlie," George said, and he put his glass down so suddenly it cracked. "What do you think you're making fool faces about?"

"Nothing," Charlie said, sobering down, and would have been all right but he glanced at Jay Clevenger, and saw such a fierce look of disapproval that he began to giggle. He couldn't stop it—shouldn't have had that Pennsylvania whiskey, was the trouble.

"God damn you, Charlie!" said George again and suddenly lunged across the table and took Charlie by his shirt. "I'll teach you to laugh at a poor girl has to earn a dollar doing dirty!" And swung back his other arm, and hit Charlie hard, right in the face. It was a hard, smacking blow, and it rocked Charlie back in his chair, and bloodied his nose for him.

"Hey, now," Clevenger said, and reached to grip George's arm. "No call to hit him."

George shook him off. "I'll hit any man who does Mary Connors harm," he said. "By bad mouthing, or anything else!" His face was red as a Yankee beet.

Charlie Potts got his bandanna out and wiped his nose with it, and some people in the place looked up to see what the trouble was.

"You're a damn bully, George," Charlie said, from behind his bandanna.

"That's right," George said, and Bergstrom brought them their drinks and set them on the table. "I'm the bully-boy of this outfit, and don't you forget it, Charlie, unless you want to try me here and now?" He drank his whiskey straight down.

"I didn't say anything about fighting you with a revolver or anything," Charlie said, blood drying on his upper lip, his face red with shame at being called down so.

"I guess not," George said, watching the back door to see if Mary was coming back inside, "slow as you are, and me being the quickest there is on the place . . ." Brenda and a man came in the back door, but Mary Connors didn't.

"Ha-ha," Charlie said, holding the bandanna to his nose again. "That's a good one."

"You said enough, now, Potts," Clevenger said. "You keep your trap shut."

"What did you say?"

"He didn't say a damn thing, George," Clevenger said. "I'm tired of you acting like some rube in here. If you're anxious about Mary, go look for her!"

"I'm not. Her business is her own."

"I'll say," Houlihan said, by the wall.

"Any bets down on the Kearney race?" Ed Cherry said. "Mike Coontz saw the Arab . . . said he looked quicker'n scoot."

"He'll bust a leg on that course," Clevenger said. "No Eastern animal can run a rough course out here. Be different on a fine track."

"They're rakin' the track," Ed Cherry said. "That Arab'll eat it up."

"Shit," George said, looking away from the back door of the Ace. "What did you say?" he said to Charlie Potts. "You saying there's a better shot than me on the Bit?"

"Charlie . . ." Clevenger said.

Charlie lifted his face out of the bandanna. His nose had stopped bleeding. "Damn right," he said.

"Charlie . . . !"

"A better shot . . . and a hell of a faster shot, too!"

George looked mighty amused. "Say," he said, "that's real rich, Charlie. You talkin' about old Leslie?"

"God-dammit, Potts," Clevenger said.

"No, I'm not, but the one I'm talking about could shoot your socks off, Peach! I saw him shooting."

"You're a god-damned liar, Charlie Potts," George said, and raised his hand as if he would hit Charlie again, and grinned when he flinched. "And if you're not, then who is this terrible fellow? McCorkle?" and he laughed.

"Not him," Potts said, and just then Mary Connors came in at the back door, with Lee Morgan. She had her arm around the boy's waist.

"God damn it," George said, as he saw them.

"There he is."

Clevenger stood up. "Charlie, you've said enough. If I hear a word more, I'm going to break your jaw for you."

"What's going on?" George said, distracted, as Mary took her arm hastily from around the boy's waist, and waved and smiled across the room to George.

Houlihan, against the wall, drained his mug of beer. "He means, it's the boy that's so terrible fast with his pistol—and more than that, it looks like."

"What the hell is this? What is it?" George shoved his chair back and stood up. He turned to Tom Houlihan. "You Mick dog-turd, I know what you're doin'!" George was shouting.

Clevenger, standing, grabbed him by the arm. "Settle down, now, boy, that deputy's over there."

John Chook was standing at the bar. He turned to look at them.

"Fuck him," George said, as Mary came toward the table, smiling, the boy walking behind her.

"You dirty thing!" George shouted at her. "You're just a stinkin' dirty whore!" He pulled his arm from Clevenger's grip, and shoved the foreman away. Then he pointed at Morgan. "I have got your number, you sissy piece of shit!"

"You get on out of here, honey—he's drunk," Clevenger called to her, and Brenda came running across the room, and took Mary's arm and pulled her away.

"Don't you run behind her, you cocksucker!" George shouted at Morgan, and took two long steps out from behind the table.

"Look out for the deputy, now," Ed Cherry said,

and got up from the table and stepped over to the wall. "No shootin'."

The men at the next table got up, too, and went over against the wall.

"Kid," Clevenger called, "you get on out of here. You go on, now!"

The boy stood, puzzled, twenty feet from the table, staring at George Peach.

"Git!" Clevenger called to him. *"Get out!"*

"You stay right there," George said, "and I'll give you your choice, you damn gonsel! I'll beat the piss out of you, right here. I'm goin' to break your goddamn jaw for you—or I'll kill you where you stand!" He had tears of anger in his eyes. "I'm going to teach you to make a dyin' girl whore for a gold piece!"

"George . . . George . . . calm yourself, now," Clevenger said, a few steps away from him. "You know better than what you're sayin'. Nobody'd hurt that girl. Now, you know Mary's a business girl, and we all care for her and wouldn't hurt a hair of her head."

George ground his teeth, and started for Morgan with his fists up.

"No," the boy said. And he put up his open hands. "I won't stand for being beaten."

"That's enough, now," John Chook called from the bar. "The both of you men sit down and shut up or get out of here!"

"You called it," George said, and stopped and set himself to draw. "You called it, you nasty pup."

"Don't, George!" Charlie Potts, too late. "Don't try him, George!"

"If you're so fast," George said. "Show it!" And his

right hand snapped down—and back up, with a cocked Colt's forty-five.

This revolver was rising to level when young Lee Morgan drew and shot George Peach through the chest, and killed him.

The bullet—the boy had fired just the one—struck George in the chest, broke his breastbone with an audible crack, and pushed him staggering back into another table, the unfired Colt's still gripped in his right hand.

He went back into that table and fell back and down in an explosion of laid-down poker hands, chips and beer glasses. People were still shouting—jumping out of the way, crouching on the floor, ducking their heads as if what they couldn't see couldn't hurt them—when it was all over, and George, rolling off the collapsing table, already dead, hit the sawdusted floor with a heavy thud and rattle as a chair fell over after him.

"Son-of-a-bitch! You—boy!" John Chook by the bar, pulling his .38 from under his coat. "You stand right there . . . you are under arrest!"

The boy turned as quick as a top, and shot Chook through his right side. The slug spun the small man full around—it had struck a rib and torn it away—and Chook's head, as he fell, struck the edge of the bar with a whack that seemed to stunned ears in the Black Ace as loud as the shots had been. The deputy fell full out, the .38 skittering away, and no-one made a sound more.

Lee Morgan stood in the silence, the Remington in his hand seeming ugly and much too big. The boy, wreathed in gunsmoke drifting slowly off toward the windows at the side, was as pale as a sun-bleached sheet. His brows and eyes and mouth looked black against the whiteness of his skin. It was odd to see his lips move as he talked.

"I'm leaving. I'm leaving here," he said. "If anyone troubles me, I'll shoot him."

Silence.

"I won't trouble you," a man, very drunk, said under a table; and someone giggled at that.

Morgan walked slowly toward the front of the saloon, the big Remington held before him like his ticket out the door.

"I won't trouble him," the drunk said.

It seemed to take a great deal of time for the boy to reach the bat-wing doors, then push them open—the revolver-barrel tapping on the right one as he did—then walk through them and out. The doors seemed to swing back and forth forever.

"Oh . . . Georgie," Mary Connors said. "Is my Georgie killed?"

CHAPTER FOUR

BRIGHT LANTERNS in the street. Four men had already carried the deputy—bleeding like a dray-crushed dog—through the shifting light and dark down the street to Doctor Nicholson's. Marshal Meagher was inside, in the Ace, looking at George and asking questions, asking where the other Spade Bit riders were.

Clevenger stood by the dark side of the building, loosing his horse's reins from the post. "You big mouth mutt," he said softly. Charlie Potts said nothing.

"I blame you for this, Charlie."

"I know it was all my fault," Charlie said, his voice sounding odd because of his bruised nose. "But George is . . . George was a damn bully—you know that, Jay!"

"Keep your voice down," Clevenger said. "You saw that boy shootin', did you? And saw he was quick? And you prodded George into it, damn you." Clevenger got his reins free. "Well," he said, "you traitor, get up on your horse and stop that snifflin'. You got George killed and you ruined the boy doin' it."

"I didn't mean it."

"Stop that weepin', you damn traitor, and get up on that horse. We have to go out and tell Missus Dowd what happened. And I'd rather be George Peach and dead, than be you the way she going to look at you."

"Oh, don't say that, Jay . . ." Charlie said, and was told to keep his voice down. "Now, don't say that to me . . ." Tears shone on his face in passing lamp light. Men were calling to each other in the street. Running in the darkness.

"Get on your horse."

Charlie got his horse's reins loose and climbed up. "You wouldn't talk so, if it was you George had hit in the face . . ."

"You follow me on, and shut your mouth," Clevenger said, and led out of town at a lope, finding his way by memory as much as occasional lamps, as fading moonlight.

Catherine Dowd stood in the moonlit shadows of her front porch, listening as Clevenger, just dismounted from his weary horse, told her of George Peach's death . . . Lee Morgan's riding out of Grover, ahead of a marshal's posse mad as fire about the shooting, additional, of the deputy, Chook-hurt bad.

She listened to Jay tell it, standing still in her wrapper, her plaid Scotch shawl. Frank Leslie stood in the doorway behind her, listening, saying nothing, leaning on his walking stick.

"But how . . . ?" she said, when Jay Clevenger ran out of words. "Why would those boys fight? I . . . I could understand if they had a fistfight over some girl . . . or gambling."

She waited for Jay to tell her why Lee Morgan had shot George, and killed him.

"Well, Ma'am . . . it was sort of over a girl . . . one of the . . . dancers, at the Ace."

"You mean one of the prostitutes, Mister Clevenger?"

"Well, that was right. That was what he meant."

"Which girl?"

"A girl named Mary Connors, Ma'am."

"The Irish girl—the sick girl?" The women around Grover apparently kept tabs on the women around Grover, whoever they might be.

"Yes, Ma'am." Clevenger was an honest man. "But it wasn't the girl's fault, Missus Dowd. She had nothin' to do with it, personally."

"I did it." The voice of Charlie Potts, from atop his pony in the dark beside the porch steps. "I chivvied Ceorge into drawin' on the kid. An' all the time, I knew old George didn't have no chance. I saw the kid shootin'; once, up in the hills."

Nobody had anything to say for a few moments. No sounds but night sounds, a restless horse neighing down in the feed lot. Might be some thrush there; Bent was drying the animal's hooves out on the loose chaff, would dig and scrape out the frogs, pour oil of turpentine down in there after.

Night sounds, some wind higher up, hissing in the darkness over the ridges.

"Charlie," Catherine Dowd said, "why would you do such a thing?"

"George hit him in the face, ma'am," Clevenger said, "and both of them was drunk."

"I won't take that as my excuse," Charlie said, out

of the dark. "I was scared to brace George Peach, so I fiddled the kid to brace him for me. I was just like a yellow dog."

Another period of quiet, then.

"Pretty smart, I'd say," Buckskin Frank Leslie said, leaning on his walking-stick in the lamp-lit doorway. "It's what I would have done when I was your age, if I couldn't handle a bully."

"You would?" said Charlie, sounding very young. His pony shifted, hoof clinking on a pebble in the darkness.

"Damn right—pardon me, my dear. Tell me, Jay, did George threaten, seek a fight?"

"Well, sir—you know George."

"Well enough. A decent fellow, but a young hard case just the same. And looking for trouble."

"But Lee," Catherine Dowd said. "That boy . . ."

"Peach force that fight? Draw first?"

"Yes, sir," Clevenger said. "I'd have to say that he did."

"And that quiet boy shot him?" Catherine Dowd.

"That boy's about the quickest with a revolver I ever saw, Ma'am. He's a real wonder, and that's a fact."

"Georgie never had no chance at all," Charlie said. "And I knew it."

"Blow your nose, boy," Leslie said. "You're not near as bad as you think you are. Took Peach's foolishness as well as your own to put him down. You're more to blame for getting that Morgan boy into a fight."

"The law will be out here right behind us, Mister Leslie," Clevenger said. "I doubt Meagher minds about George that much but he sure was hot about Morgan shootin' John Chook. Says he's goin' to hang him."

"Oh, dear God."

"Now, sweetheart, I doubt that Meagher will catch that boy. Jay, what horse was he riding?"

"Fandango—and he's all right, but nothin' special to go."

The horse neighed in the feed lot again, and they heard an answering neigh . . . the sounds of hooves coming up through the home pasture to the south.

"The law's here, sure enough," Clevenger said.

"Charlie," Frank Leslie said, "go get your roll, take a fresh mount, and head on up to line. You ride fence up there by the Old Man 'till we call you in."

"No, sir. I'll stand up to it."

"You will do as you're told—and you'll do it damn quick! We won't wash Spade Bit laundry in front of half the trash of the town. Now—git!"

A silent Potts wheeled his pony and trotted off toward the bunkhouse.

The hoofbeats were louder, a dozen horses, at least. They could hear bit chains jingling.

"They'll want to search the buildings, Mister Leslie . . ." Jay Clevenger, wondering if he were to see more shooting.

"Let 'em—if you don't object, my dear?"

"No," she said, "I don't care what they do. But, Frank, that poor Morgan boy. And poor Charlie . . ."

Lee Morgan had ridden hard in the moonlight, but he had not ridden far.

He'd forked out of Grover at a hard gallop, letting the Bit horse find his way through the dark streets, the mud-rutted alleys. Lee had wanted nothing but distance, distance from the Black Ace, from Grover, distance above all from the memory of George Peach's face, struck from fury into agony and death, all in an instant.

Lee had come a long way, months before, to get to Grover, and then out to the Spade Bit. Had come a long way before that—a long way to grow up, and not an easy way, either. But he hadn't had to use a gun. The pistol skill had been something else, something special . . . for another purpose entirely. Not to be used in common quarrels, or for gain, or to frighten and bully other men with, either. That remarkable skill, natural to the boy as breathing, and then refined by endless hours of practice, was meant for something more serious than a saloon room fight.

It had come as a shock to Lee, being forced to use that skill, being left with no choice but to use it—or to die.

Everything spoiled, he felt. Ruined now. And by that, he was not considering his current flight, or the trouble with the law sure to be following hard on his shooting of that deputy, Chook. The law, which had never taken shooting lawmen lightly, took it even harder now, with civilization slowly cramping in on the western frontier.

They'd be looking for him, and not only in this territory.

But all that seemed unimportant to Lee Morgan. Something quite beside the point of many lonely years. The only vital thing about it, aside from that territory change in George Peach's face, was that it would almost certainly stop him from doing what he had planned since he was twelve years old.

He reined the brown in, and stood in the stirrups to look back along the track. The mountain meadows, high in fresh spring grass, shone dull green in the moonlight. The pines, clustered thick along the upper run of the Little Chicken, showed black.

There was no sign of following. Not yet.

Lee turned the horse's head north. He was on Broken Iron, now, and would be for another hour and more. Then, a little before dawn, he'd reach Spade Bit. There would have been time and to spare for the law to have come and gone, looking for him.

The last thing they'd expect, would be his showing up there so late, so many hours after the shooting. Doubtful they'd leave even one man behind, to wait and see.

And if they had? Well, it would be just too bad for that fellow, and that was all there was to it.

If someone—some odd stranger, say—had appeared now to Lee, and asked what in blazes he intended, going back to the Bit to pick up his horse (granted it was a fine, nervy pinto, and better than the cavvy-plug he was riding), Lee would have been left short of an answer. It was the pinto, of course, but it was also something more. A loneliness, perhaps, a need to say goodbye to a place that had been his home for many months.

A need, perhaps, to consider for the last time, that other matter. The reason he'd ridden into the country.

The place was asleep.

Lee sat the sweating, tired brown on the ridge above Spade Bit, and looked to the east for the first lighting streak of dawn. There was no such sign. The night, now the moon was down, was dark as roofer's tar, and dawn still a piece of time away.

Lee kneed the horse out at a walk, heading down the winding track to the headquarters buildings, to the stable past the south corral. In a few minutes, he'd be on his way again, gone west with the pinto fresh between his legs. It would take a posse and a half to catch him up then, before he cut the skirt of the mountains, and got to the railhead at Parker.

Have to sell the pinto there—and a shame it would be to do it. But the day was gone a man could ride away from the law over territories and states on nothing but a fast horse. Good days, and gone. The telegraph and the sheriff's posses that sprang up along the wire's route made that kind of run a fool's play these days. No—it would have to be the train, and the crowds and confusion of the dozen towns and cities along its route.

Lee had never had to run before, but he was no fool, and had thought about it—though for another reason than he was running now.

Odd about the fight at the Ace. It seemed, hour by hour, to be more and more a dream. George's shouts, his furious face—jealous of the girl, Lee supposed, and must have been mad drunk to have called him out over it. Furious face—and a quick draw. Not fast enough, though. It was the strangest thing how slowly every movement went. It had seemed to Lee that the whole world had started moving slow as molasses for those moments. Except for him.

Poor George had had no damn chance at all. Lee felt obscurely bad, guilty of taking advantage, somehow. Not his fault, though. Not his fault . . .

He rode past the corral at a slow walk, worried

that the fice might wake and come out barking and bawling 'till he recognized Lee. And that would be too late.

But the dog slept. And so did the rest of Spade Bit. It seemed a ghost ranch in the faint starlight. Even the wind was still.

A horse nickered in the lot, and Lee reached down to cover his own mount's nose, to hush a reply. No lights. No lights in any of the buildings and sheds. One man would be with the mares in the east quarter . . . Bent, likely.

At the stable, Lee swung off the brown and led him in, staring hard to make out the way through the dark, now wanting to trip over a shovel or shit-fork . . . make a racket. He remembered just in time, and walked a wide circle in the gloom around the stallion's stall door . . . heard the shift of great hooves . . . saw, or thought he saw, a dull gleam of the big horse's rolling eye.

The pinto had been stalled at the far end of the stable. Lee found an empty stall two doors down from that—led the brown into it, and, fumbling in the dark, unbuckled its bridle and tugged it off—un-cinched the saddle, heaved that off and lugged it and bridle out of the stall, swinging the door closed behind him with his foot.

Lee carried the saddle and bridle down the passage to the last stall, pursed his lips, and whistled softly to let the pinto know it was him.

"*Took you long enough.*" And with that amused voice, the sudden bright flare of lamplight.

Lee spun—the Remington magically in his hand—and saw Frank Leslie, smiling, standing across the passage, a kerosene lamp flaring on the top plank of the stall beside him.

Leslie was leaning on his stick, eyebrow raised at Lee's draw. "That's a nice quick draw you have there, boy," he said. "Peach had no chance against that, I'd say—if you can shoot to match it."

For Lee, it was as if a dream had turned to nightmare.

"You . . . you better not try and stop me . . . you son-of-a-bitch!"

Leslie's eyes narrowed. "Now, that's a rough way to talk. I don't recall you and me falling out, son."

Worse and worse. "Then . . . then what the hell are you doin' here?" The Remington felt awkward in his hand; he put it away.

"Oh, I've been on the jump, myself. I thought you might come by for your pinto . . . and your possibles. Maybe to say so long to the place? It's hard to leave a place you lived in, sometimes."

"Not too hard for you," Lee said, and regretted it.

Leslie straightened up at that, his gray eyes darkening. He took a limping step toward Lee, staring at him hard. "All right, now," he said. "What the devil do you mean by that?" Leslie was not a young man, and was limping and unarmed. But somehow, he did not seem unarmed.

Lee's heart was pounding in his chest—harder than it had when George Peach had called him out.

"Nothing," Lee said. "I didn't mean anything by it."

"Don't lie to me," Leslie said, standing close. "What's your grudge, boy? It's something personal, isn't it? Something between us." He stood silent for a moment, looking into Lee's face. "Did I kill someone you knew?" There was a wry twist to his mouth. "A member of your family?"

"Yes!" It had burst out of Lee Morgan like water from a broken pot. "You damn sure did kill somebody I knew! A member of my family . . ."

"Boy, those things—"

"You killed my *mother*—you dirty son-of-a-bitch!" The Remington was out again, and in the boy's hand, and it shook like an aspen leaf.

Leslie took a step back. "I never shot a woman in my life."

"You didn't shoot her." Lee's voice was shaking as much as the pistol. "It would have been better if you *had* shot her—better than leaving her alone 'till she couldn't stand it anymore!"

"Who the hell are you talking about, boy?" Paying no attention to the revolver, now.

"My mother, that's who. *Beatrice Morgan.*"

Frank Leslie had never been hit harder—not by any bullet that had struck him, or by any horse kick, either. He took the blow without moving, and seemed still to be staring at the furious boy before him—but he wasn't.

He was seeing, instead, other mountains in other country—a deep, wide valley carved by a river they called the Rifle. It was a long look—a look back down the years . . .

A small mountain ranch along the river . . . a whorehouse . . . a huge brute of an Irishman. He'd pulled a Colt's Dragoon to make his try and died there, crashing to the floor of the whorehouse bar. A knightly rescue, that had been. A thin dark-eyed girl, a prostitute the Irishman had been bullying . . .

Leslie had taken her back up to the ranch . . . *Lee*, he'd called himself, then. Of course—it was what she'd named the boy. *Lee Morgan* . . . Of course.

There'd been that killing . . . and another. And a hell of a fist fight with that Englishman. And then the shooting that tore it . . . that set him on his way again, wandering.

No choice, it had seemed then, but to get the hell out of the Rifle River country—to leave the small ranch, and the Appaloosas, to Beatrice . . . for her freedom, for a new start.

She hadn't told him about the coming child. Too proud, likely. Sad little girl, to be that foolish, and that proud.

"I didn't know," Buckskin Frank Leslie said to his son. "She never told me she was carrying. And there were good reasons, damn good reasons, for my going."

Poor as it sounded, it was the simple truth.

Poor as it sounded . . .

"You're a damn liar . . . you're a son-of-a-bitch!" The boy was beside himself with rage, tears of rage in his eyes. Yet made no move at all to use the pistol in his hand.

"Oh, I'm a son-of-a-bitch, all right. No doubt about it. But I'm not liar. Never was." Leslie stood studying the boy. *His son.* Now, reminded of her, he could see something of that sweet, loving girl—surely the oddest of whores—in the boy's face. His eyes.

And, of course, he'd come looking when he'd heard of the shooting . . . heard that Buckskin Frank Leslie was still alive . . . was out at Spade Bit ranch, just past Grover. Sixty miles from Boise.

Had heard, and come riding. To see his father?

More likely to kill him. Boy may have come by some of that gun speed naturally, but he damn sure practiced for the rest. Poor George Peach accidently got the benefit. And now, it looks like the boy isn't going to kill me, after all.

"I'm tired of you waving that revolver at me, son." A cruel use of the word, but needful. "Either use that piece, or put it away."

Maybe a mistake.

Lee Morgan's face went white—a look that George Peach had seen. The deputy, Chook as well. The big Remington steadied the muzzle leveled on Leslie's heart.

Most men, then, would have let well enough alone, would certainly not have pushed it. Leslie did—and for two reasons. The first was simple bad temper, a dislike of being threatened by anyone, for any reason. The second reason was cloudier, less substantial . . . a feeling that the matter had to be settled, brought to a head once and for all.

And now the time.

"How did your mother die, Lee?"

Then there was that moment's pause in the world's business that Frank Leslie recognized of old, and he thought the boy would shoot him. *Poor Doc Nicholson,* he thought. *Poor Catherine. All that work wasted . . .*

He waited in flickering lamplight for the bullet.

It seemed a long, long wait. The boy's deadly face . . . the revolver muzzle . . . the warm smells of the stable . . . the horses.

Then the Remington's muzzle slowly, slowly tipped up. The boy eased the hammer down. Staring at Leslie, looking surprised at what he was doing, the boy put the pistol back in his belt.

"I can't kill you!" Lee Morgan said to his father, startled by that odd fact. "I can't kill you . . ."

Leslie said nothing. He'd been as close as close can get; and that told on him, as the back shot the Porter girl had put into him had told. *I'm running out of sand, for sure,* he thought.

"She hung herself, out in the shed," the boy said. "I guess she ran out of wishin'. She used to think you were comin' back." He turned to his pinto, stroking the animal's smooth spring coat. Then he bent to pick up the saddle from where he'd dropped it to draw. "I was twelve years old when she did that. She left me a letter. Said she was sorry . . ."

Yes, Leslie saw how it had been. A boy left alone—blaming his mother, more than likely, for taking such a way to leave him. Blamed her—but couldn't blame her. Had to blame someone else—and that man well deserving blame. Poor Beatrice. She should have told him about the child; he would never have left her there, alone but for the old man—Bupp. And the Indian boy. A long, long time ago.

"Whatever happened to old man Bupp?"

The boy left off cinching his saddle, glanced at him. "Mister Bupp's dead. He died of a pneumonia." Bupp. That old man . . .

"Tom Cooke? The Sandburgs?"

The boy seemed surprised he knew those names . . . was asking about them. Those names, those men, were part of *his* life, not his father's.

"Tom Cooke and Jake are all right," he said. "Mister Sandburg's dead. *Shokan* fell with him. Jake and me are . . . sort of partners."

Shokan. The great Appaloosa's name moved something in Leslie that even poor Beatrice's death had not. Memories of the trail he'd ridden to find and buy that perfect horse. His name had meant *The-house-that-runs-with-you,* in Nez Perce. *Shokan*—and another word or two Leslie'd never got straight. A good name for him, too. As big as a house, damn big for an Appaloosa. Comfortable as a house, too. A wonderful five-gaited horse. Comfortable—if he let you stay on him.

Leslie didn't ask if the big horse was still alive. Wasn't likely, not after all these year. No more questions, then, about years he had no claim, no right to. Those were the boy's years, some of them without his mother—and all of them without his father. But he had kept his mother's name—long after he must have seen the ranch deed, with "William Franklin Leslie" scrawled across it.

No more questions. Rather, Frank Leslie stood silent, and watched his son saddle a horse—and watching him, remembered the boy as he'd been all these months, working Spade Bit with the others. Odd moments, casual "Good-mornings," all seemed quite important now, He had the damnedest notion to take the boy into the house, wake Catherine, say: "Catherine, my dear, it seems that young Morgan" —how could he have been so stupid as to miss that name, and with the "Lee" in front of it! Stupid. And stupid to miss the look in the boy's eyes. Well, to say, "Catherine, it turns out that this boy is my son. Let's get us up a hell of a breakfast, and sit and talk about it 'till noon."

By God—he'd like to do it!—and would, too, if the damn fool boy hadn't shot the poor bully and Chook. Now . . . now, there would be no time. No time for that. No time for anything. The boy was his son, sure enough. It needed not much more than this damn fool killing to prove it.

"Listen to me," he said to Lee Morgan, as the boy began to lead the pinto out of its stall. The boy stopped, and looked at him. "It's way too late, and too little time, for me to start playing the Daddy with you, and I won't do it. But, still, it's only fair I give you what I can, even if only advice." Having said that much, he paused, thinking how best to put it.

"Son," he said, "I lived in the best days of guns—and I was one of the best with guns in those days. And I tell you, it all came to bad—for me, and for those who cared for me. Most of the men I killed would likely have been my friends, but for a foolish quarrel, or one drink of whiskey too much. All that came to nothing. To no pleasure at all. And so I'd tell you, even if the times hadn't changed a bit. But they have. In a few years, there'll be no more living by a gun—unless you're some thief, or a thug in a city. . ."

"I know all that," the boy said, and looked at him cold as winter, "but I guess Marshal Meagher and the law will give me a few years' run." And he led the pinto down the passage and out into the yard.

Leslie had brought the boy's possibles' sack from the bunkhouse, and now he picked it up and limped down the passage after his son—afraid the boy would just ride away . . . would ride away without saying anything else to him.

But Lee Morgan must have felt something of the

same, because when Leslie limped out into the yard —to see the streak of dawn paling to the east, hear the first throat-clearing noises of McCorkle's rooster —the boy was waiting, astride the pinto but not spurring out.

Leslie went up to him, tossed the heavy sack up to him and the boy, always quick of hand as a cat of paw now fumbled and missed it, and the sack fell open in the dirt, spilling out a folded shirt, a worn bar of brown soap, and what looked like the fat black coils of a snake.

The boy started to swing down, but Leslie bent over and scooped the sack up, putting the shirt and soap back into it. He held the coils of black in his hand. It was a whip—a "blacksnake," and a beauty.

Strange—he'd never seen the boy using it, chousing stock. Strange. Leslie weighed the thing in his hands. Then he realized what it was for.

"This was for me, wasn't it?"

Lee stared down at him from the pinto's saddle; there was light enough now for Leslie to see the boy's face quite clearly.

"Yes," Lee said. "That was for you. I was going to whip the skin clear off you, Mister Leslie." The "Mister Leslie" hurt Frank as much as the whip might have. "And I would have, too, but you were hurt too bad, and didn't go armed."

Leslie handed the whip up to him. "Here, you'd do better to kill a man, than use that thing on him."

"I'll remember that," the boy said, turned his horse's head, and started to spur him out of the yard.

"Wait!" Wait for what? What the hell had he to say to the boy, beside, *Wait just a minute, now—so that I can get a better look at you . . . so that I can remember you . . .*

The boy had reined in . . . was waiting for what he he had to say.

"If you get into a tight," Leslie said, "something worse than this business—and you can believe me, there are worse tights than this—then you come back here. You come straight on back here, and we'll stand together."

Damn fool thing to say . . . the boy would think he was an old jackass . . . Damn fool thing to say . . .

Lee Morgan didn't answer. He turned, spurred the pinto, and rode straight out of the yard without looking back.

Leslie watched the boy ride out past the feed lot, and then cut off the track into the deeper darkness under the loom of the ridge. The dawn was flowing into the country, but not soon enough for Frank to see his boy riding under the ridge.

He walked slowly back to the house, missing his stick as he walked—must have left the damn thing in the stable. He was tired, and that was the truth. Damn tired.

It was morning for sure, now. Behind him, he could hear McCorkle singing in the cook shack, singing *Lorena*, the old Rebel song, during the war. McCorkle might have seen the boy ride out, from the cook shack. If he had, he would say nothing about it.

Too late to get back to bed, now. Just about time for Catherine to be getting up, making hot chocolate for the two of them. He'd tell her about it. Not much he kept, or wanted to keep, from Catherine.

Strange, though . . . when he did tell her about it

—while they were sitting out on the porch, drinking that fine hot chocolate—well, it was an odd thing, but damned if she didn't seem to have known it already.

CHAPTER FIVE

"I'LL GIVE a hundred-fifty, kid—and not a red cent more." The dealer was a tall, bony man, who wore a suit as black and dusty as an undertaker's. He was slightly deaf, and shouted somewhat in consequence.

"A hundred-fifty."

"No," Lee said, and leaned against the livery office door, rolling a Durham smoke.

"You won't get a better offer than that for that horse, I can tell you," the dealer shouted. "Nobody but a drover'll ride a pinto for a horse. Or an Injun'll do it, but that's all."

Lee didn't say anything to that.

The dealer sat behind a cluttered pine-plank desk, rocking way back in a straw-bottom chair. Lee could see a stock pen through the dirty window behind him. The dealer sat pursing his lips as if he'd said what he had to say. Nothing to add. After a few moments, he leaned over to the side to spit into a dented brass spitoon. Then he rocked back. Nothing to say.

Lee smoked his hand-made, and waited the dealer out.

"A hundred and fifty!" the dealer shouted. "That's

a wore out horse you got there! Damn plug is half dead! Have to doctor him . . . feed him a month before I can show him to a soul. That's a damn half dead horse!" He looked furious, scowling at Lee, as if —if he could be bothered with it—he'd get up and come over and thrash the tar out of him for so mistreating a poor animal. And a sad plug at that, mistreatment or not.

Not for nothing had Lee grown up on a horse ranch. He leaned on his door frame, puffed on his cigarette, and had nothing to say.

"If you don't have nothin' to say—then why the hell don't you take that crow-bait, and mosey on out of here? I'm a busy man!"

Lee shrugged, eased off the door frame, and walked out of the office and down the steps. The pinto—looking a bit peaked, it was true—was tied to the rail there.

Lee went to him, loosed the reins.

"ONE SEVENTY-FIVE!" The voice came booming out of the office door above and behind him. "AND NOT ONE GODAMNED PENNY MORE!"

Lee ducked under the hitch rail, went to the pinto's side, and stepped up into the stirrup, to mount.

"TWO HUNDRED DOLLARS, YOU GREEDY THING!" The dealer stood in the doorway above him, champing his jaws like a wheel horse.

"Deal," Lee said to him. The pinto was worth thirty-forty more than that. Fifty more if it was rested, primed and fed out. But he didn't have the time to fool with it. Had the money—he'd found two month's wages in gold in a little leather bag at the bottom of his possibles sack, and knew who'd put it there. Had put it there before she knew a damn thing about his being anybody's son. Lee had wanted to send the cash back. Might have, too—a year or so back. Not now. Was in too much of a tight, for one thing, was a year past being a boy, for another. He'd keep the gold, and spend it. It was just from Mrs. Dowd.

Not from his father.

"Gold—not greenbacks," he said to the dealer. The bony man stared down at him, champing his jaws. Then nodded. Lee had a good notion what the man had in mind for the pinto. "That there's a genuine Injun war horse, Mister. Yessir! That li'l beauty'll run all day and tote all night and kiss your mouth in the mornin'. Don't get horse flesh like that out of a leaky livery! Nossir! That's high plains' stock, with a bottom on him like an iron fry pan. Pinto? Hell, man! ain't no rider who *is* a rider forks a shit-brown or tar-black! It's pintos, for the real horsemen!"

Something on that order—and likely made the sale. And wouldn't be cheating by much, either. The pinto was a prime mount.

Lee stripped his saddle and bridle, and held the horse by its short mane for a moment, leaning against him. "So long, Whiskey," he said, and stroked the soft coat under the animal's throat. The pinto rolled a big brown eye at him, and Lee pushed him gently away and into the rope bridle an old black hostler was holding for him.

The dealer came rattling down the steps with a small handful of coins, and a piece of paper. "Can you write, drover?"

"Better than you, I suppose," Lee said, and the dealer grunted and held out the paper, and a wet-nibbed pen plucked from behind his ear.

Lee smoothed the paper against the flat top of the stair rail, and wrote: *Sold to J.D. Mullen (dealer) this day 2 April 1893 — a prime pinto horse "Whiskey." White ground, brown patches. White hoof left fore. —Lee Leslie.*

He handed it over, having signed it with a name he'd rather not. No use spreading "Lee Morgan" over Parker for the law to nose out. Now that it was done, though, he wished he'd signed something else.

Lee took the coins from the dealer's long-fingered hand, handed over the bill of sale, hoisted his saddle and bridle onto his shoulder, and walked out of the livery without looking back. He didn't care to see the pinto led away.

Parker was a railroad town, and a business town, and busy. Lee had never seen such crowded streets—neither in Cheyene nor Boise. Mostly city men, too. Clerks and storekeepers they looked like, and mighty preoccupied hustling about the streets, and ducking in and out of store fronts and offices and freighting cubbies. Most dressed up in fine store bought suits, and low shoes. As he strolled, bent a little under the saddle's weight, Lee saw some drovers and farmers going by, and ladies shopping with baskets on their arms. But businessmen predominated, as Professor Riles would have put it in the classroom of the Cree County Normal School and Academy.

"A decent *gymnasium* education, Master Morgan —to be, I'm certain, wasted on a horse-driving young fool!" Professor Riles hadn't cared much for the mountain country nor for the raising of livestock

as a fit profession for a man, or boy, who'd proved reasonable at Poesy, History, Ancient and Modern, Rhetoric—Primitive, and Arithmatical Functions.

Beatrice Morgan had been ambitious for her boy, anxious that he somehow rise above the grim and wearing realities of the frontier. When Lee'd finished the regular few grades in the Cree one-room, he'd been going on twelve—a nice, bright-minded boy, Miss Storch thought. Beatrice had not given Lee one winter of freedom thereafter, but had driven him down the valley to the normal school—nothing much, to be sure—a log house, two out-buildings, a library of four hundred and seventeen volumes, twenty-three students and Gregory Chambers Riles, a graduate of Brown University in the State of Rhode Island.

Lee had fought his mother over it—at twelve, he was the youngest student at the school, but Beatrice had visions of him as an attorney or physician, a man with clean hands—not beaten and broken-nailed, black with dirt and bruises. A better man, perhaps, than his father—whose hands had been clean enough, to look at. She might have had dreams of Frank Leslie coming back, coming home some day, to find a fine straight boy (an attorney, or physician, say) who would stand before this prodigal as a living witness to Beatrice Morgan's love.

Beatrice, exhausted by this and many other dreams, had walked out to the stable one morning, without really giving it much thought, scribbled a letter to her son and Jake Sandburg, folded it, put it in her apron pocket, and hung herself from a cross-tie beam in the stable ceiling with a length of harness rope.

Lee had come home for her funeral, stayed a week, and, perfectly free to avoid it, had returned to the Academy thereafter. It was a debt he felt he owed her, and paid for another year thereafter. Almost fifteen years old, Lee felt his debt had been paid. Riles had granted the interview, insulted him as a puppy and a fool and wished him well, in his fashion.

"If you ever do grow up, Master Morgan, and can afford the fees, I will welcome your return. Startle you though it may, you have not quite learned all there is to learn—nor all that even this primitive institution has to teach." The Professor had paused to relight a dead cigar. "There are few things or objects or individuals more dangerous, chancy, and less useful than a half-educated boy, and such you are. Be careful in trying to *think*, Master Morgan—you have the brains, and the aptitude, but not, alas, sufficient experience at it. Beware . . . *thought*."

It seemed to Lee, stomping along a planked boardwalk under a hot spring sun, humping a considerable saddle, and in momentary fear of some fat-belly deputy coming down upon him as a murderer, that perhaps he had not *thought* enough. Surely, the crippled-up gunman who'd called him "son," had handled him smartly. Brushed the Remington aside like a summer fly on a watermelon slice, handed him up his blacksnake whip like a cup of coffee, with advice stirred in, told him to come running if he needed his nose wiped—and seen him on his way.

So much for great imaginings of revenge and murder—poor George Peach had been an accident and nothing else. Lee Morgan, who had damn sure known who'd killed his mother, had met the fellow, worked his place (or Mrs. Dowd's, which amounted to the same), then made a mess in a saloon, talked to the fellow, and ridden off to catch a train.

How Leslie must have laughed, to see him go—to have seen him imagining he was something special, the only by-blow Leslie had left with whores (face that truth, at least) or farm girls, or saloon queens or whatever. Likely a half dozen of "Lees" and "Lee-Anns" scattered about the frontier. Some of them must have tracked him too, and come visiting in their time—and been smiled at, and cozzened, and sent packing.

The professor had been right. He wasn't ready for thinking—nor serious, long-headed thinking. Not yet. Damned if he could see, though, what he might have done to get George Peach off his back in the Black Ace—or what had boned George so hard to begin with. Would like to have seen the professor handle old George. By giving him Latin declensions, maybe, or a broad quadratic.

The noise of Parker was as forceful as its crowding. People seemed to be chattering like bluejays out of every doorway—shouting also, if they had any distance at all to talk over. Any space over three feet seemed to call for shouting. Lee was a young man of the countryside, and, bar a noisy saloon once a week, and a single visit each to Butte, Boise, and Cheyenne, not used to the sheer volume of sound a busy town generated on a busy day.

And it was hot—the weary end of a long ride and a steep trail. A considerable part of which had been spent looking back for dust—the sort of dust, say, that a dozen posse men might make, springing them hard with their rifles already out.

Lee's neck was still a trifle stiff from looking back.

Old lard-bucket marshal Meagher—who'd deputied for the man Leslie had killed (and looked to be getting away with killing, too, thanks to the Dowd's fancy lawyers in Boise)—had seemed a fairly comic figure, strutting the streets of Grover in his swallowtail coat and bright brass buttons. In Lee's imagination, as he rode, the marshal had seemed less funny—a lot less funny, with armed men riding with him, and one of them carrying a fine length of rope along, just in case. That bunch in imagination or in the saddle, were not comic.

It had been a tiring ride and not only for the pinto.

Lee looked for a place to rest up. But something else, first. He looked for a kid. And after two or three more minutes stomping along the boardwalk, finally saw two of them—truants sure—scooting along the street's dry ruts, accompanied by a fighting bulldogs, chalk white and earless.

"Hey—you kid!"

They both turned on a dime, looking to see if an officer or other officious grown-up was after them.

"Hey—the both of you! Come here!"

The boys, eight or nine years old, had seen weary drovers before and, staring hard to make sure Lee wasn't nasty drunk, they slowly came across the street to him. The dog lolloped around them as they came, in slow, muscular, white circles.

"What d'you want, Mister?"

"I want an errand run," Lee said, out from under the weight of the saddle, "and I'll pay a dime to go, and two-bits on the finish."

"We'll do her!" the quick one said, a slight boy with one milky eye and one sound. The other boy, larger and slower, looked up at Lee on the boardwalk, and said nothing. Perhaps shy. The dog ran under the walk on an errand of its own, the boys not seeming to mind.

Balancing the saddle—nudged, and none too gently, by the townspeople crowding past him and his saddle and his possibles—Lee dug in a trouser pocket for a dime, found one, and tossed it to the boy who'd spoken up. "I want you to go to the station, kid, find me the time of the next train west, and buy me a riding ticket on it." He dug deeper, for one of the dealer's coins, tugged it out, and tossed it down. "What's your name, boy?"

"Micky," the milky-eyed boy said, peering at the gold coin with his good eye, his head cocked like a curious bird's. Lee supposed he didn't see many ten dollar pieces.

"Micky what?"

"Micky Sims!" the boy said, surprised that Lee didn't even know that.

"Well, Micky Sims," Lee said, and he looked around, "see that ken across the street?" There was a sign of a bull, painted blue, and bat-wing doors.

The boy nodded. His friend had gone under the boardwalk, likely after the dog.

"Well, now, you go get that ticket for the very next train, mind!—and then get right on back here to that saloon and bring it to me. You do that, I'll give you a two-bit piece additional to that dime." He gave the boy as hard a look as he could, with the saddle weighing on him sore. "If you don't come back with that ticket, and the change from that ten dollar piece, then I'll come looking for Micky Sims—and I'll find him."

The boy seemed impressed. "Oh," he said, "I'll do

her, Mister." and took off at a fair clip for the far corner, barely missing being run down and killed by a furnishings dray in the middle of the street. The other boy, larger and slower, emerged from under the walkway in pursuit, fearful of losing his portion of the dime and two-bits, and hauled away after his friend, the dog galloping leisurely behind.

Lee crossed the street, taking some care of the traffic, turned to watch a spanking team go trotting by, a neat dude with the ribbons, and beside him, a lovely, long-faced blonde girl in a blue-flowered straw hat. She was that rarest of creatures, it seemed to Lee—as much as he saw of her—a nice girl who looked as fleet as a dasher. Lucky the dude on the ribbons, unless he was her brother.

Lee crossed, climbed the steps to the boardwalk, and carried his saddle and sack down the walk to the Blue Bull. With considerable relief, he pushed through the swinging doors and out of the heat and sunlight, into coolness and shade, and the smell of sweat and beer and slices of cut onions stacked beside the free lunch at the back.

He found a small beer-wet table down past the end of the bar, got to it, dropped the saddle and possibles sack on the sawdust beside, sat down with a grunt of relief, and waited to be served some free-lunch and a schooner of beer.

It took the waiter a while to get to him, the place starting to crowd up with the noontime bunch, and the waiter, a knobby man named Sessions, not used to serving dirty drovers sitting at tables on the gents' side of the bar.

It took him a while, therefore, but he did get to it. Lee, as it happened, did not mind the wait; he was pleased enough to sit in the cool dimness, watching the clerks and what-not come tramping in in their shiny shoes and checkered neckties, and line up at the bar with their friends, and joke and jape, and order cocktails made of some of this, and some of that. He saw a couple of men with pistols under their coats, but most of the Blue Bullies went unarmed, or so it seemed.

So, he didn't mind the wait, and greeted the waiter in a friendly fashion, and ordered a corned beef sandwich, a pickle, a piece of pie, and an ale-beer, frosted.

"Cost you a quarter to sit at that table, kid," the waiter said, when Lee was finished talking. "Above the cost of the beer."

"Now, why is that?" Lee said. "That seems a little high just for sitting."

The waiter sighed. "This is a gents' saloon-bar; that's why. Most workin' stiffs stand at the brass."

"Well," Lee said, "this is one stiff that's sitting—and damned if he will pay for the privilege." He said it in a pleasant way.

The waiter shrugged, turned his head—looking—and then made a sign to someone along the crowded bar, jerking his head to beckon them over.

Lee watched with interest, and saw a small bald man ease out of the crowd and come toward him, eating a hard boiled egg as he came.

"What's up, Mark?" he said, strolling up to the table. He had a husky, wheezing voice, and he had to raise it to be heard over the noise in the place.

"Don't want to pay table rates." The waiter looked down at Lee with some satisfaction.

"I hope you haven't forgotten my order," Lee said

to him, but the waiter didn't say anything.

The small bald man finished his hard boiled egg, and stood relaxed in a cheap striped suit, looking Lee over. Lee looked back, and saw that the man was a fighter, or had been. His round head was slightly lumped, here and there, and his eyes, otherwise blue and gentle, were sunk in old cushions of scarred flesh. He was not big, but he had the relaxed air of a man of competence, in a familiar situation.

"Son," he said, "I'm not as young as I once was, and it would cost me my job if you was to short pay for where you're sittin'." He smiled in a winning way. "Now, I'm supposed to be the house bully and bouncer but, tell you the truth, I'd rather stand you a beer than fight you. You look pretty handy, to me." He smiled and winked at Lee in a most friendly fashion.

Lee nodded, listening, and the small man seemed to find that encouraging. "Tell you what," he said. " 'Stead of you an' me scramblin' all over this here dirty floor, now, an' spoilin' our clothes—why don't I buy you a drink over at the bar, or anyway, a beer. An' Mark here'll haul your lunch over to you nice as can be. What d'you think of that?"

Lee, who had not forgotten Chook falling—and likely killed—who had not forgotten marshal Meagher and the telegraph lines either, had not sent a kid to the station to get his ticket for him only to draw the law down after all with a shooting. He prepared to accept the offer, as sensible.

And would have, but for two things. First, the waiter's face, already sneering . . . already seeing Lee's back-off. And second—and a lot odder—some muddled notion of what his father would have done in this situation. He was puzzled by the very idea of caring what his father would have done, and was on the balance, when the waiter tipped it.

"Up an' outta there, kid," he said, and waved his small white towel in dismissal.

The bully, no fool, gave the waiter a quick cold glance, and set himself for trouble. This might be seen only in an appearance of greater relaxation, as he eased his shoulders in the jacket of his suit.

"Now," Lee said to the fighter, "listen to me. I will not fist fight against you; and I will cause no noise or trouble in here. Just tell this piece of snot to bring me my lunch, and not to spit in it on the way. I pay no extra fare to sit at a table, and I'll kill you or any other man who lays a hand on me." That said, he leaned back slightly to clear the butt of the Remington, and smiled up at the fighter in a friendly fashion.

The bully, named Bob Clay—and once, as Clay McKeon, a successful welterweight—had lost none of his brains in the ring. He'd listened carefully as Lee talked, and watched the way he'd sat and settled back when he'd finished talking. He'd noticed that Lee spoke tonier than your common drover, had had some schooling. He'd noticed the boy was easy, and had cleared some room for a draw at his revolver.

The boy had confidence. That was the word for it. He was easy as if he'd a dozen friends sitting beside him. Clay had met that kind of easy many times, in the ring. Had had it, himself in fact. He recognized it, and thought that the boy had certainly used that revolver, and knew how to use it. The boy was also a stranger; and that was most important, because it meant he would likely be moving on, and could thus be left off where a local man might have to be called, so as not to be suffered in the future.

These judgments, natural, not even put into words, Mister Clay weighed to his decision.

"O.K., kid," he said, pleasant as ever. "We don't need such a bad fuss in here as that." He turned to the waiter, who he blamed for forcing the matter with his mouth, gave him a look, and said: "Feed the kid, Mark—don't table charge him." He winked at Lee again. "And don't spit in his lunch."

"Thank you," Lee said, and meant it, and the small bully drifted away to the bar with a wave of his hand.

Lee'd finished his sandwich—which was mighty fine quality for a free luncher and was just tucking into the pie, a mollasses and pecan confection, and sweetly good, when he saw the milky-eyed boy come shifting through the legs of the men packed in along the bar. The dog had trailed on in behind him—no trace of the bigger kid—and was the object of several men's attention as they tried to chase him out, but circumspectly, due to his remarkable collection of muscle and teeth.

Young Master Sims spotted Lee—his head cocked to the side as he identified—and trotted on over, leaving the dog to manage on its own.

"Say, Mister," the boy said. "I got your ticket," and waved a long narrow strip of complicated yellow paper. His other hand stuck out at Lee palm up, with a sweaty wad of greenbacks in it, salted with loose change.

Lee took the ticket and noticed the last town stamped on it was just short of the Oregon Territory.

(West, indeed.) The ticket had taken most of the ten and entitled the bearer to nothing but "an accomodation for travel," which, Lee supposed, might be anything from a regular bench seat to a pile of hay in a cattle car.

Lee separated out a two-bit piece, and a dime extra, and left those in the small dirty palm. "When's the train pull out?" he said.

"Three-thirty-four, exact." The urchin said. "Mister Brennan said so."

"He the dispatcher?"

"He's the engineer!" Micky Sims was startled at Lee's ignorance, and Lee felt something old-fashioned, talking to a boy who likely cared more for railroads than for horses.

"That's the time, is it?"

"It sure is, by Mister Brennan's watch." The boy stared at Lee for a moment—he hadn't thanked him for the extra dime—and added, "It's a Waltham."

"What?" Lee said, getting back to his pie.

"Mister Brennan's watch," the boy said, stuffed his two-bits plus a dime into a side pocket of his dirty trousers, and trotted off across the sawdust, ducking in and out of the patron's legs and collecting his dog, without a word or sign, on his way out.

Lee glanced up at the big clock hanging on the wall by the saloon doors. It showed just before one o'clock, and already the lunchtime crowd was starting to thin a bit, the clerks and storekeepers heading back for their counters and cash drawers, full of beer, eggs, pigs' feet, and as many sandwiches as the bartenders would let them cadge off the lunch.

There had been, all along, barely heard under the gabble of talk and laughter, and shouted orders for beer or whiskey or cocktails, the slight, ringing click and clack of billiard balls in play toward the back of the place. Lee'd never had much luck at billiards or set-up pool, but there was no reason not to try his luck again, in a reasonable way—and it seemed a better time-waster than humping his saddle about the town, or, for that matter, leaving his goods with the barkeep and strolling the town to see the elephant. Some description of him had to have passed by telegraph now. Be his stupidity, more than bad luck, if he were taken by policemen while shopping the windows.

All in all, he thought he'd try his hand in the back, among those town sports free enough of employment for an afternoon of leisure. He finished the last bites of pie, and last swallow of beer, picked the ticket up, folded its considerable length, and tucked it into his vest pocket, stood up, and bent again to have his saddle off the floor.

The barkeep—a fat citizen with a fine mustache—accepted the saddle and bridle and sack with a grunt, threw back the trap, heaved them through and dumped them on the duck-boards beside the cooler. "Here when you want 'em," he said, and glided on down the bar to draw four beers—all bunched in his large white fist—and slid them even further down the mahagony to four men who looked like bankers or lading clerks, anyway.

Lee walked on back to try his skill against the sharps of Parker, Idaho.

There were four tables deep in the gloomy back of the Bull, each with a tin-shaded kerosene lamp swinging over the green felt, the clean, shining whites and reds of the balls.

Regular games were going on at three of the tables, and some wagering along with them. A few men sat in high-legged chairs aginst the south wall, watching. It was dim enough, what with dirty windows and cigar smoke, for the cigar tips to glow as they puffed them. Their eyes were shaded by their hat brims.

Lee looked for an empty chair, figuring to watch a while, find out how fierce the competition was going to be—and wouldn't have to be too fierce, at that, to clean his clock. But while he was standing, gawking around for a cane-bottom, someone called out, "Say there, cowpoker!" And Lee saw a short, plump fellow in a yellow suit crooking a finger at him from the fourth table, the furthest, over by the back door. There were only the plump man, and a tall, handsome boy—a farm boy by the looks of him—playing there.

"Say, cowpoker! You lookin' for a game or a dame?"

That got a chuckle from the men in the chairs, and Lee headed back to the table.

There, the plump man held out a soft square hand with rings on it, and Lee shook it. "LeMar," the plump man said; he was very neatly dressed. "This young man is Bengst Torsen." The farm boy gave Lee a shy nod. "I do hope, Mister . . . ?"

"Leslie. Lee Leslie." Damn. He'd have to do better than that.

"Well, I do hope, Mister Leslie, that you are a betting man?"

"To a limit," Lee said, and LeMar laughed.

"Well, none of us can bet the sky," he said, "that's everybody's limit." He gave Lee a sly look. "Now, for example, I might tell you that I play the game of pocket billiards—some call it 'the pool'—for the pure rare fun of it! But if I told you that, young man, you'd say, 'this fat sissy is trying on a fast one, and that's a fact.' " He spun his cue stick as he talked. "And, my dear boy, you'd be absolutely right. For I, with my young friend, Benny, here, am a shark—a sharper, a rag, a tout. In short—I make my living at it." He looked at Lee to see what he would say to that.

"Well, it's honest of you to say so," Lee said, and found the fellow likeable.

"Just the reply we wanted—not so, Benny?" The farm boy whose hands, now that Lee got a better look at them, were too soft and cared-for to be a farm boy's, kept his eyes down, shyly, and nodded.

"Because, my handsome young drover, that reply means that you will play us anyway. And for money!" He stepped closer, and smiled up at Lee like a girl—smelled like a girl, too, at least a fast girl, who used perfume. "You see, I've just told you that we'll cheat you if we can and out-play you if we have to! And all for money—no sport to it at all. And do you walk away? Do you offer to punch me in the nose? An unwise proceeding, anyway, since my young Swedish friend is armed, and temperamental."

Looking more carefully than he had before, Lee saw that the Swede had a small revolver tucked into the hip pocket of his overalls. The boy ducked his head, and grinned at Lee in an embarrassed way.

"You see?" the plump man said, skipping away from Lee and around the table to pick up another cue from a rack against the wall and toss it lightly across the table. "Catch! You see, I've found—*we've* found, that honesty is indeed the best policy. Marks are never happier than when they *know* they'll be cheated! We've found that it's the worst thing in the world to try and fool people. They don't like it, and they don't like to pay for it." He was setting up the balls as he talked, his pale, plump hands flashing under the lamplight and disappearing again into shadow.

"Shall we play a nickel a point?" he said.

"Ya," the Swedish boy said. He had a big man's baritone voice.

"No," Lee said, "I won't pay you. But I'll pay two dollars for a lesson in pocket billiards."

The plump man's hands stopped dead on the bright-colored balls. His astonished face dipped down into the lamplight. "Good God Almighty," he said. "Common sense! And at your age!" He fluttered his eyelashes at Lee. "Shame I'm already in love . . . you're a rare one."

"T'ree," the young Swede said, sounding less shy.

"Three dollars it is," Lee said, and chalked his cue.

Two hours later, Lee straightened up from the table, easing his back. His eyes felt dog-tired from staring at the bright balls, following their bounces and angles, and damn sure his back was weary, bending over the table edge to watch and shoot. More watching than shooting, as it happened. "You watch us, now and practice what we show you on your own time," Mister LeMar had said, and begun a lesson of degrees. Degrees of angles—it's all geometry and experience, LeMar had said—and degrees of human foolishness, fright, greed, and pride. Mister

LeMar had taken it all, shot by shot, and shown it, shooting—playing first the fool, then the tout, explaining how people—like the balls of the game—could be set up, positioned, shot and pocketed.

"Oh, there's a lifetime of learning in this, my handsome boy," he'd said, "and you're getting only four dollars' worth."

"Three."

"Oh, was it three?" He was demonstrating how, even in a game they could not afford to lose, a rube's attention would wander for something as silly as conversation, his concentration fail . . .

"Don't believe for a minute," LeMar had said, sometime later, "that there's a secret to any game except practice, avoidence of error, and a knowledge of your opponent's weakness. Hold those three aces in your hand, and you win more often than you lose. Simple."

And he showed Lee how to take a sure long shot over an almost certain short one. "They don't call this pocket billiards for nothing. It's pocketing that wins."

Just after two hours had gone by, before Lee had to call the lesson to catch his train, LeMar had put an end to it. "For two reasons . . ." he'd said. "First; you're beginning to think of something else—which is beginning to waste my time. And second, you don't play well enough—dare we say 'yet'?—to learn any more. You owe me three dollars."

The Swedish boy, who'd only helped set the balls up, held out his hand for the money, and Lee counted it out. He felt it was very well spent. In the last hour, more and more men had gathered at a distance from the table to listen to Mister LeMar, and to watch. LeMar, aware of this larger audience, had raised his voice accordingly, and made a few more jokes as he'd played.

The lesson over, the three dollars collected, the plump man had smiled at Lee over the table, and said, "Now—the graduation examination. Graduation from the first grade, of course. Young Mister Leslie: What is *my* weakness as a billiards player?" And waited, no longer smiling, for an answer.

Lee thought about it, paused, and thought some more.

"Well—" he said, "you like to show off, so I guess you care what people think of you. And if you're worrying about that, I suppose it must hurt your game . . . maybe only a little . . ."

Mister LeMar said nothing for a moment, then he said, "Out of the mouths of babes . . ." and reached into the inside pocket of his suit jacket, took out some greenbacks in a money clip, peeled off three singles, and handed them over to Lee, stretching across the table to give them to him. "My last lesson," he said, "and this one is free: You never teach, but you learn."

Lee had shaken hands goodbye with Mister LeMar, and with the Swedish boy, gone up front to the bar for his saddle, bridle, and possibles, and toted them out through the bat-wing doors and into the bright light and heat and dust and noise of the streets. The barkeep had told him the way to the depot, and Lee started the five block walk that would take him just past it, so that when he cut back uptown, he'd be by the shanties alongside the tracks, not at the depot itself. He had no intention of standing at the station inviting a policeman to come and question him. Even a stupid law officer would have a man by the depot for a few days, looking for a lean young man, more a boy than a man, with dark blond hair, light brown eyes and a Remington revolver stuck in his belt.

It was a hike, and—not the first wrangler or drover to do it—he cursed the discomfort of high-heeled boots on a walking man. Late in the afternoon though it was, and hot, mighty hot for a spring day, Parker still had streets seeming as crowded as Chicago's. Damned if Lee could figure what there was to keep so many so busy. The railroad, he supposed, must make as much work as it brought in goods and took them out. Looked bad for the times to come, he thought, tramping along the boardwalk. The more railroads, the more bustle would come with them. Be hard to find a peaceful place in a few more years of railroading, he thought.

Of course, he wasn't used to it. No railroads had ever bothered to drive a line through Cree County. It was still horses for speed, and wagons for lading, up there. Seemed to give people more time to breathe, he thought. Maybe not so much money, though. Maybe left them a little dumb for want of something new. Since the rustlers had dried up in the mountain country—and since those weeks that Buckskin Frank Leslie (ah, not easy to forget all the talk about him) had shot the poop out of a bunch of people . . . an old man, for some reason or other, an Irish ruffian . . . another man . . . and the town marshal, Tod Phipps. Bunch of people remembered seeing that fight—didn't have much to talk about but all those old killings. Shootings damn near twenty years ago, and damn fools still talking about them . . .

Confess it, though, nothing much had happened in Cree County since. About the most startling thing being Mister Martin the draper marrying Mrs. Boltwith. That had been news for a year, up there, those two old things getting married. Talk about your strange couples . . .

He made the five blocks, though almost foundered, then cut north along a street called Seventh, and walked up that 'till he got to the end of the street, which was a dirt yard dead end backed by a set of small slat shacks. Naked kids were running in and out of them, and one woman, looked Chinese or something of the sort, was sitting on a one-step stoop staring at him.

She stared at Lee as he walked across the yard, bent a little under the weight of the saddle and possibles sack, and walked on past her and into a narrow alley spoiled with what seemed to be people-shit and dog-shit run together. Some dog shit for sure, because a bunch of them, fices and mutts, came running around a shed corner and came right at him—most to bark, but one or two to bite at him. Lee kicked them away, but the one or two came right back, and the brown one, a big dog, bit at his leg and tore his trousers there.

Lee still had a way to go—he could see the stretch of track ahead, the depot building a ways further down. Too far to go, and too many minutes still to wait to be letting dogs jump around and bite him. Too near the damn depot to fire a shot.

He kicked, and cursed—and the dogs barked and yelled and the same one or two would come on in and try and bite him. And not one damn person came from the shacks to see what was what.

Lee was hot and dusty, and tired of lugging, and the brown dog—who limped, but wasn't slowed by it —rushed in on him and seized Lee's foot as he kicked out, and put a damn hurtful bite on it. His teeth went through the leather. Truth to tell, it scared Lee a bit. There were enough dogs in the pack to chew him up. And no shooting.

He threw the saddle and bridle down, swung the possibles sack at a hound of some kind that jumped up at him, showing its teeth, and then wrenched at the tied neck of the canvas bag, yanked at the bow tie knot and pulled it open. He reached in, felt the fat coils of the whip, and tugged it free.

The long, long, thin-braided length of leather, black as soot, oiled and supple as a woman's hair, came free and uncoiled and swung and hissed and sang in great quick loops through the air.

Most of the dogs, all too familiar with the whistling sounds of whips and quirts and sticks, and hissing of flung stones, sprang back, but the brown dog, the fierce biter, furious, rushed in again, and Lee, shortening his stroke as a drifting sheep herder named Robinson—a new Zealander, who had described whalers to Lee when he was thirteen, and still horse-mad—had taught him, caught the leaping dog a shocking crack with a whip loop (not even the murderous tip, knot-braided, with a tiny tag of hammered tin) and knocked the breath out of him. Lee reversed the long whip-butt in his hand, stepped in, struck the dog across the muzzle with it, and sent him careening away, howling, the others following after, tremendously excited.

Lee was glad to see them go. His foot was paining

him, and the notion that the brown dog might have been mad with the rabies, crossed his mind.

He coiled the whip, stuffed it back into the sack, and heaved his saddle up onto his shoulder again. It was a short walk up to the rail embankment, and a shorter climb then to the rails. Lee stood well to the side, on the wide edge of broken ballast rock, and looked down the track for the train.

He could just see it, stopped, its stack barely smoking, alongside the depot. He could only see the front of the locomotive. There was a slight curve in the track running down to the station. A good distance away, too; Lee doubted anyone at the depot would take notice of a fellow by the tracks so far away.

He looked back for the dogs, but they'd skidadled. The whip, which he'd practiced with as tediously as he'd practiced with the Remington, had, in fact, come in handy a time or two, dealing with stock—and once, galloping a raiding coyote down, and breaking its neck, running, with the lash.

It had been intended for Leslie, of course—as, Lee supposed, the Remington must have been. Certain sure he'd lashed enough branches—shot up enough stumps—and all of them with Leslie's imagined face. A hard, sneering face . . . the buckskin jacket—which Lee had never seen the man wear around Spade Bit—that Bisley-model Colt's people talked about.

The real man—the actual Frank Leslie, had been a considerable shock. Older, for sure . . . damn near an old man, was the truth. Wore out, too, he'd looked—and busted up bad by the back shooting and, likely, by the wounds that Pace had given him.

Frank Pace. That was a name—had been a name to conjure with, Professor Riles would have said. They'd heard of *him* up in Cree County. The local ranchers sometimes talking of hiring him on to "clean up the trash," by which they meant small holders and the few sheep people. A name to conjure with.

And Frank Leslie had met the man face to face, shot it out with him in the Grover House dining room (where Eastern writers still came to stay and see the spot) and killed Pace dead, taking two dangerous gunshot wounds while doing it.

Lee was aware—and had made the small fighter at the Blue Bull aware—that he was no "slouch" with a revolver himself. Was, in fact, mighty fast—and a good shot, to boot. Still, though, he was not the equal —not yet, anyway—of what his father had been . . . what Frank Pace had been, either. Those were grown men, fighting men who'd met and killed more than a dozen, maybe two dozen other fighting men. Guns, fists, and knives. Indians . . . hard-rock miners . . . railroad gandies . . . rustlers and Texas drovers . . . pimps, and paid gunmen and murderers.

No, Lee Morgan of Cree County, Montana, had a long, long way to go, and maybe a dark way to go, before becoming a person that famed, that dangerous. Leslie had told him in the stable yard that it wasn't worth the doing, that it always came to bad.

Likely, the man was right.

It occurred to Lee that if he got off this trouble, it might be well to put the Remington away—the whip, too—and call his wild oats sowed and done with. Why do a thing, if it brings no pleasure? He'd certainly had no pleasure in killing poor drunk George Peach. Pushed or not, it had been perilous close to a foul deed: he had known full well how fast and handy George had been with a pistol—and that not fast enough, not handy enough to take Lee on and put him down. He'd known well enough—been tempted a time or two, when the boys were practicing, to step out and show them a thing or two . . .

Close to a foul deed—and would have been, if George had left him any room at all. The deputy? Well, the man was intending to arrest him. It was something Lee couldn't have stood; it wasn't in him to put himself in people's hands like that. He didn't feel sorry.

Trouble enough for a lifetime, though. And maybe trouble *for* his lifetime, if that deputy died. That might leave him no choice. Frightening, that a few moments shooting in a small saloon could so mark a man . . . determine the whole rest of his life.

Might be best to dump the Remington in a pond, and let all that go . . .

Soon, perhaps . . . soon. But not yet.

The train's whistle suddenly echoed down the track, and Lee could see a darker plume of smoke puffing up from the stack. Getting ready to start. He picked up his saddle and sack, slung them both over his left shoulder, to leave his right hand free. He was a little worried about catching on to the train while it was moving—had heard that tramps and drifters sometimes caught and rode moving trains. It seemed, though, that it might be difficult, with a saddle and other possessions slung on your back.

He felt in his vest pocket with his free hand, making certain his ticket was safe. Surely they wouldn't go to throw a man off just because he boarded out of the depot? Lee thought not, but he'd only ridden on railroads a couple of times, and wasn't sure what rules this line might have. He did know the high and mighty railroads could pretty much do as they pleased. "A remarkable collection of deliberate criminals," Riles had called the railroad barons, "and certain to rob the people blind."

The train's whistle sounded again and, staring hard, Lee could see that it was starting to move; he saw the sun flash on some brass fitting as it slowly began to come along, faintly heard a harsh *chuff-chuff* as it gathered steam.

The track rails beside him began to hum, and, out of curiosity, he bent and put his hand on the nearest, feeling a subtle, deep vibration through the steel.

The locomotive was moving faster, now, seeming to get bigger as he watched. The steel rail shook under his hand. Lee let go of it, and stood up, getting the saddle back in balance on his shoulder. The train seemed to be coming at him mighty fast, almost as fast as a man could run, it seemed. He could see the long side-piston, the big black driver-wheel spinning faster and faster as it took the long slight curve away from the depot, and came straight toward him, black smoke now billowing up out of the stack.

He didn't see how he would be able to catch hold of it, not without running alongside, at least. And, thinking that, Lee turned and began to trot down the side of the tracks, his boots crunching in the loose ballast-rock, the saddle jouncing on his back, his possibles sack swinging in his hand.

Damned if he could see how he would do it.

A whistle came screaming out behind him, and

Lee, breaking into a clumsy run, shied like a young horse. The engineer—what in hell was the fellow's name?—must have seen him, be warning him off the tracks. Lee glanced back over his shoulder, and saw the sunlight reflected in the locomotive's huge round light, sparkling off its polished steel and brass bright-work. The rumble of its wheels was lost in steam hiss—clouds of steam boiled out of machinery along its sides. Lee saw the name *Western Flyer* in gold gilt paint along its side, high over the whizzing black circle of the drive wheel.

Then it was beside him—a blast of heat and noise and wind. The ground was shaking under his feet. Lee swerved away, staggering a little under his load, and saw the engineer staring down at him as he rolled by. Then the coal car, painted-up like the locomotive, went grinding past him—and the next car came, going by faster and faster. Lee thought he saw faces at the small windows, and forced himself to run in closer. The platform at the end of that car went past before he could reach out for it; he gritted his teeth and forced himself closer, forced himself to run faster. The next car came rumbling—and something on it just touched him—only touched his right shoulder, and Lee tripped and stumbled, out of balance under the saddle. His boots slipped on the loose rock and he fell to one knee and, scared of falling under the wheels, made a desperate effort and jumped to his feet running, gasping for breath, his heart pounding. The next car came and slid past him, its wheels pounding on the rails.

"Stick out yore damn arm!"

Lee looked to the train and saw, almost even with him, two rough-looking drovers leaning way over the platform rail, their hands stretched out to him. Beneath their hands, in the massive shadow of the car, the great wheels squealed and ground gleaming along the track.

Lee turned, and with all his strength, ran into the side of the train.

The drover's hands caught at him—he felt the saddle lift suddenly away, smelled hot grease and machine oil, the noise of metal bearing weight—another hand, very strong, seized a handful of his hair, then another hand at the upper part of his right arm. They were pulling him up—dragging him hard against a steel railing. His boots kicked the air, and the railing was at his belly—his shirt tearing—and he was upside down and dumped with a thump onto a floor of steel that shuddered beneath him. His saddle and possibles were dropped on top of him.

"Welcome, stranger!" A long, wind-and-whiskey-reddened face, silvered with beard stubble, grinned down at him. "Boy—you shore better be hell on a hoss 'cause you ain't shit mountin' a railroad train!"

"Haw-haw!" A second face, round and red as a harvest moon, loomed over him. "Ah think the kid's done pooped his pants, Larry!"

"Git up, boy! Come on, git up!" Whiskey breath blew warm into Lee's face, and he rolled out from under his goods, got to his hands and knees, and then stood up, balancing himself as the platform shifted, rose and fell slightly with the pitch of the road-bed.

"You was damn near killed, kid!" the man with the long face said. He looked to be a Texican drover, as did his friend, broad as this man was tall. They wore dirty checkered shirts, and canvas pants, dark yellow, criss-crossed by Mexican *buscadero* belts sporting a brace of Colt's each in low-slung holsters. They wore big Bowie knives in their boot—the boots high-heeled as a flash whore's evening shoes—and broad brim high crown hats with one brim-side pinned up. Their hands, one pair bone and rawhide, the other pair beef, were, both sets, as large and worn as shovel blades.

The men had blue eyes—a light, pretty blue—lumped and bone-broke faces, and a number of teeth gone missing.

Texicans, for sure. And merrily drunk.

"Welcome to the 'Flyer,' kid," the broad one said.

"Thanks for hauling me up," Lee said, and held out his hand to shake. The drovers shook his hand in turn, very solemn, and hurt the bones in it.

"Why in hell didn't you git on at the station, boy? Some gal's daddy after you?"

"Sure hope not," Lee said. "I never said I'd marry her!" and bent to pick up his sack and saddle while they laughed. "Thanks again for hauling me up."

The tall one reached into his back pocket, and pulled out the remnants of a pint bottle of whiskey. "Don't run off, boy. Stay an' have a snort!"

Lee was tempted—damn sure felt the need of a drink, but the Texicans were half-drunk, now, and hard enough to miss stone sober. They'd be making some kind of fuss sooner or later, looking for a fight, or bothering some woman, or lying down to sleep in a train-car aisle. Lee didn't need that kind of notice. Didn't want any notice at all. And might already have made a mistake letting people see him running like a fool to catch on to a moving train. Could've been less noticed at the depot, after all . . .

"No, thank you," he said. "Truth is, this railroad

train is moving around a little bit too much for my belly's good!"

"Shit—bes' thang in th' world for yuh!"

Lee grinned, shook his head, and backed through the platform door into the relative quiet of the car. The last he saw of them as the door slid shut, the tall drover was tipping the bottle back for a long drink; the broad one stood patient as a bull in pasture, waiting his turn.

People turned to look at him as he backed into the aisle, saw nothing remarkable except a young fool who'd nearly missed his train, and went back to minding their own business. Lee stepped sideways down the narrow aisle, looking for an empty seat, and trying to keep the saddle's furniture from knocking some passenger's hat off as he went. A young girl in a gingham pinafore giggled, watching him inch by.

Most of these people were nicely dressed—damn near all the men had button-up suits and hard crown hats on, and fine shines to their shoes. "A boob in high society," Professor Riles had described a fellow out of place. Lee was feeling a bit of a boob himself, lugging his leather and possibles along, his right trouser leg near bitten away by that damned brown dog. Wished he'd caught him with the tip, now!

Craning his neck, Lee thought he saw an empty place beside a fat woman in a blue-striped dress and bonnet just four seats down. He started to hitch along a little faster—and damn the passengers' hats—when he felt a man's hand at his shoulder. For an instant, Lee almost dropped his luggage and tried for a draw at the Remington. Then he saw the railroad badge on the man's hat.

"Put that truck down, Mister—" a querulous voice, not the Law—"and hand me some sort of a ticket, or by Tophet, you'll be gettin' off as snappy as you go on!"

It raised something of a laugh.

Lee stepped back for a bit of room, bent, and set his stuff down. Then he dug in his vest for the ticket, pulled it out, and handed it over.

The conductor seemed a little disappointed to see it, unfolded the narrow length, and perused it carefully. "Oregon?" he said, and gave Lee a look, as if to say "and good riddance,"

"That's right."

"Long haul," the conductor said. He was a man in his fifties, nice enough looking, except for a blotch of red birthmark on his throat. Looked as if he'd had his throat cut. He took a silver punch from his back pocket, punched three or four quick holes along the length of the ticket, and handed it back to Lee.

"Better get that truck out of the car aisle, boy. Can't be blockin' any aisles. 'Gainst company rules." Having done his punching and said his piece, the conductor eased past Lee and his luggage, and went on down the aisle and out the door to the platform and the car beyond it. Lee heard him say something to the two drovers, and their laugh, just as the door slid shut behind him.

Yes, sir—had got on this train entirely inconspicuous, to use an Academy word for it. Entirely inconspicuous.

Now that he was free to go to it, Lee saw that the place next to the fat lady was taken by a kid who had to be the fat lady's boy; he was round as a baseball and popping his buttons.

Lee sighed, steadied himself as the train took a lurch, bent and picked up his goods, and headed for the next car up front. He got through the door, across the platforms—one old farmer standing out there in the wind, puffing on a pipe—and into the car. And there, right past the door, he saw a place on the aisle. A seat beside a sleeping wire drummer. The fellow had on a brown suit and fine fur-felt Derbie hat, and a twist of Glidden's three-spike stuck through his lapel, to let people know what he was peddling.

Was a time, a few years ago, that buttonhole would have earned him a beating, some parts of the country.

Lee shoved the saddle and sack down in front of the seat—let the fellow step over it, if he must—and sat down himself, with a geat deal of relief. He was dog-tired—no funning intended—and hog-dirty, and wanted nothing but to sit. He stretched his legs as well as he could, and tried to ease the kinks in his muscles. Still felt as if he was carrying that damn saddle. One shoulder'd probably ride higher than the other forever. Never feel about a horse the same, now, now that he knew how they felt with that leather on their backs, to say nothing of a fat-butt on the leather.

He looked around, as much as he was able, through a high set of bird feathers in the hat of the woman sitting just in front of him. Every color of the rainbow, those feathers. There was one looked just like a flower.

He glanced past and saw a man at the far end of the car standing at the water bucket. Fellow'd just dipped himself a long drink, and Lee watched him swallow it. Appeared that he'd have to get on up, after all, and go and get a drink himself; he felt thirsty enough to take the whole bucket on.

While he was thinking that, the man turned to get back to his seat—caught Lee's eyes on him—and stood dead still, staring back, swaying easily with the motion of the train.

He had a look as blank as a sidewalk, dark eyes. He wore a neat duck, dark suit—looked like a fine one—and a clean white collar and cuffs. Natty and neat. Small man with a fair-sized nose, mustache to go with it, and dark hair oiled fine and combed flat.

Lee let his gaze drift off—if the man had a case of the stares, or liked to look people down, then let him do it. Last thing he needed, was for some snotty banker's clerk to come down the aisle asking was he looking for a thump on the nose.

In a while, he'd mosey on up for some bucket water and be sure and not notice that little gent when he did it. Could be some sort of deputy, but he surely didn't dress that part. A snotty clerk or manager, was more like the thing . . .

Lee sat in comfort, riding the slight motions of the train, hearing, above the quiet talk around him, the rumble of the wheels . . . the distant *chuffing* of the engine . . .

It was enough to send a man asleep.

CHAPTER SIX

LEE WOKE up with a jolt—echoing the train's own jolting as it rumbled 'round a long curve in the road-bed, slowly climbing.

He glanced around, and saw that the wire drummer was still snoring softly—fellow must have a bottle about him, to sleep so heavily. Lee looked past the man, out the side window, and saw a sweep of rain, a long curving range of thunderheads way off across the prairie. The darkness was coming down with the rain, the storm coming down early. As he watched, the first fast patter and spatter of raindrops struck across the glass, streaking the dust in long wavering finger-marks, then, in a rush, flooding it away. He heard the rapid murmur, then the pattering rush of rain striking the railroad car's metal roof. It drummed deeply over his head as the rain swept over.

The conductor was coming down the aisle with a long, thin brass-oil lighter, a small flame wavering at its tip. Reaching over the passengers, he lit the wick of each small gimbaled oil lamp along the side of the car. In the deepening gloom of the storm, the interior of the car gradually took on a red and golden light, soft and flickering, as the conductor moved along.

Lee was very thirsty, had to take a pee as well, so he stretched to ease his cramped muscles, and then got up and went down the aisle, now enjoyed the swaying, rocking motion as the train rushed along. Must be something like being on a ship at sea, he thought. It seemed to be easy enough to get used to, even with a road-bed this bumpy. Times he'd ridden trains before—on shorter trips—they'd seemed to run a lot smoother.

He squeezed past the conductor as the man came down the aisle holding his lamp-lighter carefully high—didn't want to set any ladies' hats alight—and walked up to the locomotive end of the car, and to the bucket and jakes.

He picked the small dipper up out of the bucket, swirled that water and tossed it down into the waste pail, then dipped it again for a drink. He emptied the dipper, relishing the chill tin-and-clear-water taste, then dipped himself another drink. He plopped the long-handled tin cup back into the bucket, and tried the handle of the jakes door. It pushed open—with no one squawking on the other side—and he stepped into a mighty cold and noisy space, full of the racket of the train, and sudden leaks of wind and water. In this narrow, slat-boarded closet, the railroad company had built a tall, square box with a tin top, and then had cut a neat round hole in that top. There was a thick sheaf of cut newspaper hanging on a hook beside the privy.

Lee unfastened his belt, and, holding the Remington in one hand, unbuttoned his trousers, pulled them and his underdrawers down, and sat down on the cold tin to feel an immediate cold wet draft that made him jump. What people meant by "roughing it," he supposed.

He had his pee—and a crap as well—wiped himself, relfecting as he did on the mess that must lie along most railroad tracks, though he couldn't remember ever seeing any manure on them when he walked or rode over tracks. Speed and weather must dispose of it . . .

He buttoned and belted up, tucked the big Remington back into its place, and pushed the door open. A stolid, square-faced woman was waiting in the aisle. She had only one bird on her hat, a brown sparrow in a cake-shaped plate of black net, and didn't seem abashed to be sharing a can with men.

Lee stepped past her and started back down the aisle, wondering about the next stop—some stop before nightfall, he hoped. He was getting damn hungry, could do with a doughnut, at least, or some sort of sandwich.

He was past the first two rows of seats, when he looked up—and directly into the eyes of the small man, the neat duck in the fine dark suit.

This small man was sitting on the aisle, at ease, his legs up and crossed on the cushion of the empty seat in front of him. He stared into Lee's eyes in the same blank, dark-eyed way. Not as if he were looking for a fight, after all, or trying to make Lee drop his eyes. It was just a look, mildly curious, like a man examining another fellow's horse, or new vest.

The small man's eyes were dark and bright at the same time. Dark in color, but shining with reflections of the lamp light. His suit, his white linen, were very fine stuff—no doubt about it. Finer than a clerk could afford, for sure.

A woman was asleep on his shoulder. Together, they had their seat and the empty seat in front of them, its back tipped over toward the front end of the car so they could rest the feet on the cushions, and some of their luggage as well.

—The woman was young, Lee thought, glancing fast as he went by—young, and a dasher, with a thin, high-bridged nose, a wide mouth, relaxed now in sleep—and freckles on her face. Lee had no time to judge her figure as he went by. Lucky Small Man, he thought. She'd had no hat on, and her hair had been dark, burnished red, like the spring coat of a fine roan mare . . .

The small man turned his head as Lee went past, watching him go by like some neat, big-nosed owl, guarding from its stump in evening woods.

Lee kept on back to his seat, passing a rough looking fellow, asleep, his head tilted back—his mouth wide open, snoring to beat the band—and several seats full of neat citizens, and, sometimes, their wives and kiddies. Most of these folks were riding along as empty faced as steers, staring ahead of them at the back of the next person's head, and thinking, Lee thought, some mighty uninteresting thoughts.

The wire drummer was awake when Lee slid into his seat beside him, and was nursing a whiskey bottle in his lap. "Want a bite?" he said. He had a pale, soft face, and dull gray eyes under the shadow of his Derbie brim.

"No, thanks," Lee said. "Doesn't agree with me."

"Don't say . . . ?" the wire drummer said, looking at Lee as if he were a specimen new in his experience. He shook his head. "Don't agree with you . . . Now, sport, that's a rough go," he said, and looked at Lee a moment longer from underneath his hat brim. He shook his head agian, brought the bottle up for a quick nip—it appeared that the Line had a rule against boozing in its cars, though not, apparently, against boozing out on the platform, at least, not when it was being done by two big, half-drunk Texican drovers, armed to the teeth.

The drummer had another quickie, then slipped his bottle under the seat between his feet. "Say," he said to Lee, "will you wake me when we get to Carruthers? If I don't twig the stop myself."

Lee said he would—never having heard of Carruthers—and the drummer, fully confident, tipped his hat down over his eyes, settled down into his half of the seat, leaning well against the wall under the trembling little bowl of the glass lamp swinging lightly on its gimbals above him, and in a minute—or perhaps less—was sound asleep, snoring, Lee noted, hardly at all. The barbed wire business appeared to be a tamer one than it had been, if this was a typical salesman for it. Might be the companies sent a tougher sort down into Texas, still.

Lee soon found himself doing as all the other passengers were, who were awake. Sitting, swaying with the train's motion—hearing the noise, the buffeting of the rain storming against rushing metal—thinking, dreaming of this and that . . . of his mother, her thin strong hands at her work around the house . . . her gentle way with horses. Boys in the town, at the grade school and, later, once or twice, at the Academy—had tried their tries at making fun of him for his mother having been a whore. Had not made that fun more than once, any of them. A boy named Bothwell, Harold Bothwell—a large, lumpy kid, pale and powerful—had said something nasty to a friend of his, about getting up the two dollars to screw Lee Morgan's mother.

Lee had heard of that saying a week after it was said, and had gone to Bothwell's house in Cree and waited outside in the backyard in the dark—watching this menber of the family and that come traipsing out to the necessary—until, shortly after moonrise, Harold came out with a candle and a handful of Sears and Roebuck catalogue pages.

Lee had met him on the walk—a handsome one, paved with brown brick all the way out to the shit house—told him what he'd heard he'd said, and waited for a reply.

Bothwell, sixteen and big for his age, said yes indeed, he'd said that very thing—and, in fact, was trying to raise the two bucks, now. He was a clever boy, and tough.

Lee had had a rock in his right hand, nearly as big as a baseball. When Bothwell'd said that say, Lee had swung the rock around, struck him across the side of his head, and put him down on the walk with a thump.

The rock had hit with a sharp, cracking sound, and Lee thought he might have broken Bothwell's skull. He didn't care. Bothwell had lain still for a moment, one of his feet trembling in a faint runner of lamplight shining from the kitchen window of the house, then he'd grunted, turned over onto his side, and from there to his hands and knees to try and stand up.

Lee'd hit him again, swinging the rock down like a cleaver at the back of Bothwell's neck, and driven him down onto his face. Bothwell tried to shout out, then, to call for some kind of help, and Lee swung the rock at him again while he lay on the brick walk, hit him in the mouth, and broke two of his teeth off, right at the line of the gum.

Harold Bothwell was a tough town boy, but he was only sixteen, and badly hurt. He began to cry.

Lee had thrown the rock away, then unbuttoned his trousers, and peed on Bothwell as he lay there.

Lee had waited for several days—when Harold Bothwell was absent from school, for a constable—Trig Jones, or Mister Patch, to come and arrest him. But the Bothwells had apprently gotten enough of the truth of the matter out of a suffering Harold, not to wish it spread around the valley that the boy had said what he'd said. And been beaten for it by Beatrice Morgan's fourteen year old son. A few years later, to be sure, respectable people moving into the valley of the Rifle River would have shunned Beatrice Morgan as a whore and prostitute and fallen woman, and would have stood by that publicly, said by their children—however crudely—or by anyone else. But, at the time, it was still early days in the settlement, and the men and women who had come first into the mountains, and had fought wolves and Blackfoot and each other with knife and pistol and rifle, had assumed a bond that held together against even the late-coming respectability that traveled smothering out of the pulpits and drawing rooms of the East.

There were a number of important citizens of Cree, male and female, whose occupations had not always been perfectly genteel. To question one of these, was to question all. Beside which, Beatrice Morgan had been a central figure—and present at the *denoument*—of the valley's great theatrical and historic event, the final, murderous appearance of one of the great gunmen of the West (and had, in adddition, born this Achilles a son.)

And Beatrice was a dear and gentle girl, and was liked.

So, the Bothwells took their son's beating, and swallowed it, and kept it in their bellies, against the time when that little hoodlum, son of worse, would get his comeuppance. The Bothwells — Mister Bothwell was the town Postmaster—certain of the future, could wait. Times were changing to their times.

Remembering this incident—and with more satisfaction, less unease than he felt remembering George Peach staggering back, death tearing at his chest, remembering the sound the deputy's head had made, striking the edge of the mahogony bar—Lee felt himself begin to drift back to sleep, barely kept awake now, by a hunger for just some snack, some candy, maybe, the sort that had been sold from trays when he took the train up to Cheyenne with his mother. That had been a fine thing. Fudge. Inch-thick squares of it . . .

Someone came down the aisle, headed front, and, lurching slightly with the motion of the train, brushed Lee's elbow with a thigh as hard as wood, and knocked it off the arm-rest.

Lee looked up as the man looked down—and saw a bark-brown face in a mask of rage. Eyes black slits so narrow the definition of the pupil could not be seen. A mouth that seemed sliced into the face with a knife.

An Indian—and huge, but dressed in a fancy white

man's suit of clothes, gray, with a fine pin stripe, that fitted one of the biggest men that Lee had ever seen. Taller than the tall Texican drover—wider than his beefy friend.

Over the furious face, the inhuman eyes, a fancy dark gray plug hat rode on midnight hair, shining with oil in the lamplight.

The huge man bent down, close to Lee.

"You disgusting white devil," the huge man said, "you child of goats—you forced me to touch you by your carelessness." He half sang, half whispered the words. Lee smelled his breath. It smelled of whiskey and peppermint.

"If I had you alone, and off this foul machine. Ohhh . . . if only I had you alone . . ." he crooned like a madman, but softly, "I would cut that white arm off, that made me touch it, and I would see you cook and eat it."

Lee's heart was pounding—his head back againt the seat. The man had scared him—hell, would scare anybody! But, as the huge face was still held lowered, close to his, glaring at him, Lee felt, with great relief, his temper rising—all the hotter for being frightened.

He took a breath, and said to the giant, as softly as the man had spoken to him. "You can kiss my white ass, Digger, if you wipe your mouth first."

The mask of rage above him froze as if a blizzard had come howling through it. A silent blizzard of deadly cold.

"What is your name, young man?" the frozen face slowly moved to ask—and, for the first time, Lee realized the giant spoke with some eastern accent—like a dude gent from a rich man's college. That prissy accent, those neat little "t's" and "s's," only made the Indian more frightening. It was as if a rabid dog, foaming, were to giggle like a child.

"Morgan . . . Leslie." God damn it—that name! Why in hell hadn't he thought of another name?

"Thank you," the Indian murmured to him, and smiled. It was not a threatening smile; it was a smile of real pleasure, and it looked very strange on his face. "Now I'll be certain of finding you . . ." He was almost whispering . . . "certain of finding you . . ."

Abruptly—as if it had not happened at all, as if there had been no casual jostle, no murderous grimace, no words spoken at all between them, the giant was straightening up and striding away down the aisle, the top of his fine plug hat almost brushing the rail-car's ceiling.

Lee watched him go, saw him reach the water bucket, and stand, swaying with the rocking of the car, dipping out a drink. His heart still thumping in his chest—still ashamed that he had allowed the man to speak that way without calling him at once, without reaching for the Remington, Lee stared after the Indian, imagining some things he might have said. Imagining what he might have done—should have done—when that red nigger had spoken so.

Watching through the lamp light and lamp shadow as the train lurched on into the storm, Lee saw the giant raise his arm for a second drink—and, with that gesture, the flap of his coat fell back, revealing the massive curved butt of a huge revolver. The piece had to be twice the size of the average weapon, and in a moment, Lee was sure it must be a Walker Colt's. A Walker—the biggest, and most powerful handgun made—said to be able to knock a range bull flat, with one round into bone.

Then, Lee almost had to smile—he saw the giant's eyes caught in a glance, obviously returned, from the seat up front where the small man sat. The huge Indian was getting that blank stare, for sure. With some enjoyment, Lee watched to see what the Indian would do about it.

He did nothing. Stared back for a few moments, then shifted his gaze and started back down the aisle, balancing against the jolting of the train. He walked past Lee without looking at him; and, turning his head, Lee saw the Indian move a suitcase off the last seat in the back of the car, and slide in, easing his bulk against the wall, deep in shadow. Lee didn't know how he'd missed him, coming into the car.

It was the damndest thing . . . try to sneak on to the train and have every person on it staring, thinking that young fool near went under the wheels! Sit tight in your seat like a prairie dog in a burrow and some fool crazy Indian, big as a house, comes along, bumps you, and says he's coming after you, for sure.

Next, Lee thought, it would be the law. A marshal would likely come falling down with the rain, break through the roof, and land in his lap. He smiled at that, then thought a while about the dude Indian—or at least he talked like a dude. Didn't look much of a sissy, though. Looked pretty damn fierce, in fact. And crazy. There were a lot of crazy people out in the mountain country—all over the west, for that matter, or so Lee'd heard. People back east let them wander away—wanted them to wander away, if they'd caused trouble. And the ones born out here tended to roam more than a bit, as well. Lee'd met them, one or two, riding alone down trails, singing to themselves some nonsense song accusing other people of this or that. Sometimes talking to themselves.

If these crazy people were armed, or looked fierce, people left them alone. If they looked gentle, then the kids would run after their horses and throw rocks at them, or some drovers, out for a lark, would rope them out of their saddles, and tie them up in a tree and leave them.

The Indian was apparently one of those—from the east, and bore a fierce grudge against white people. He looked damn fierce—and was heavy armed, to boot.

Lee couldn't see where such a brute, a crazy Indian, had gotten such fine clothes, had been done up so neat he could have passed for a society man in New York or Boston, if it wasn't for his being so big, and an Indian.

Lee thought he might be some chief from back there who had sold a parcel of land. He also thought the man might have been drunk. Would explain all that peppermint he was blowing out, making all those soft voice threats. Could also mean it had just been the whiskey talking, that Lee wouldn't have to worry about the bloodthirsty redskin coming after him because he bumped his leg on Lee's elbow.

Damn foolishness.

Couldn't say a train-ride was a bore, though. No sir, couldn't say that. What with little beady-eye, up front with that looker and something belonged in a circus sitting in the back of the car, wearing a fine gray plug hat.

Couldn't say it was boring—but it damn sure made a person hungry . . .

* * *

Lee woke to a change of motion in the train. It was slowing. He heard the distant squeal of brakes, then felt the thump as their car's brakes were thrown, and heard steel keen on steel right beneath him, loud enough so that the woman sitting in front of him reached up to cover her ears with her hands.

Stopping for what? The rain still fell, Lee thought more gently, but still coming down. And when he looked out the window—the wire drummer was awake, but nodding, staring dully at the back of the seat ahead of him—Lee saw that it was full dark, for sure. He dug for his watch, a one dollar Sears and Roebuck Elgin, and read just past seven o'clock by the dim light of the oil lamp overhead. The watch was usually within ten or fifteen minutes of true, and Lee figured the real time had to be after seven, for it to be so dark out there, storm or not.

The brakes squealed again, and some big piece of machinery thudded into place just under Lee's seat. The locomotive whistle sounded up front, loud enough to rattle the glass in the windows.

The train was slowing to a stop.

Past the drummer, who now seemed to have nothing to say—looked stone-plastered to Lee—he saw a row of lights, lamps hanging along a shed roof.

The rail-car bucked a little, then groaned to a dead stop.

"Carruthers," the wire drummer said. "This is where I get off." He sat there for a few moments more, however, his face pale as marble. Lee had never seen a man drunker, who still had his eyes open. But the drummer could hold it. He grunted something to himself, and suddenly sat up straight, then heaved himself to his feet and sidled blindly over to get to the aisle. He stepped all over Lee's feet doing it, and Lee wished for a moment it was that crazy Indian being stepped on—serve him and this drunken fool right.

"Say, pal," the drummer said, from the aisle, "how's about handin' me my case, huh?"

Lee bent down to wrestle the drummer's sample case from under his seat—there were two empty bottles down there—passed that over to him, and then, seeing a carpetbag on the rack above the oil lamp, reached it down for the man, and handed it out to him.

"Thank you, very much," the drummer said. "You're a good kid." Turned, and weighted down with his goods, walked stiffly down the aisle along with several others getting off the train at this stop.

Didn't seem like much of a stop. Lee leaned over to look out through the rain-spattered window, and could make out a loading dock and a couple of sheds. Likely a cattle shipping town, and not much else. Stock yards. Fair enough stop for a wire drummer, at that.

He stared out a moment longer, feeling a little odd in the train's stillness, its new lack of motion. Just as he started to draw back—thinking to ask if there was a place for eats in Carruthers (if they were going to stop long enough for that)—he saw some men. Five of them, standing in yellow slickers in the rain. They'd walked out of a shed, and were standing, talking, in the lamplight. They had rifles.

The smallest of them, an old man with a big mustache, had a badge pinned to the lapel of his slicker. The brass shone in the lamplight.

Well—they hadn't quite fallen through the roof

and into his lap. But they'd done well enough.

It was strange, Lee found, how great a temptation it was to do nothing at all, to sit still and wait . . . to imagine they were just riding the train to get somewhere else . . . to imagine they were after someone else, had never heard of Lee Morgan and a deputy shot so far back along the line—and further than that, back into the country.

It was a great temptation to him, not to do anything at all. Just . . . wait.

He got up—seeing the five men already moving along the platform toward the end of the train—and reached down for his possibles sack. The saddle would have to stay—and a damn sixty dollar Brazos double-rig, too! He'd head up toward the locomotive—maybe put the Remington on those people up there, make them pull out with the law aboard, while he took a jump for it in the fuss. Had to be some kind of a horse for sale—or steal—in the damn settlement.

He went up the aisle fast, feeling the better for moving, and took thought of the big Indian. That fellow'd have to wait for another day for his fight.

A few strides short of the water bucket, Lee heard a sudden gust of rain come down fresh. The storm was not played out yet. It would mean wet riding for him—and poor tracking for the law. Well enough.

Then—just as the sound of rain came, and he thought that thought—something caught him by his right wrist. It was such a hard hold, Lee thought for an instant he had somehow hooked his wrist on the steel frame of a seat-back or something of that sort. It swung him half around, his wrist held hard—and then he saw the hand, and fast as he could, went for the Remington left handed.

"Calm yourself, boy—I'm not the law." Said softly. The hand, square, stub-fingered, kept its grip, stronger than any man's had a right to be. The small man, immaculate in his dark suit, his snowy collar and cuffs, smiled up at Lee in the friendliest way. Lee had his left hand grip on the pistol, but he didn't draw it.

"He isn't, really." The woman was awake, sitting up and yawning like a kitten. "You can believe Harold—about that."

"Sit down, boy," the small man said, and suddenly let go of Lee's wrist.

"They've left a man by the locomotive," the woman said, looking out the window. She had large, clear hazel eyes.

"Sit down, boy," the small man said, staring up at Lee, "unless you were just going to the jakes. You weren't just going to the jakes, were you?"

"Heavens, Harold," the woman said, "will you try for a little conduct? Your language!"

The small man smiled. "She puts me over the jumps, don't she?" he said. "Now you better sit on down here—unless you didn't bump a deputy down in the hills back of Parker. Did you?" He leaned forward to pat the cushion of the empty seat facing him. "Or aren't you a kid called Morgan?" He patted the empty seat again. "Aren't you?" The small man cocked his head, and Lee heard the same sounds—voices down past the end of the car, the sounds of boots on the metal platform. "You can run, if you want," the small man said. Other passengers in the car were stirring, looking back to see what the commotion was, peering through the lamplit gloom. The rain was rattling on the roof like sticks on snare drums.

Lee dropped his possibles sack, and kicked it under the seat. Then he sat down facing them.

"Stretch out, now, at your ease, Kid Morgan," the small man said, his stare as dark, as blank, as encompassing as before. "We heard all that talk at Parker . . . and I thought about that—and here comes you, a kid and nothing else but, and running for the train like a nickel tramp."

"Have some supper?" The woman had tugged a wicker basket out from under her side of the seat. She lifted it to the cushion beside Lee, and unfastened the lid. "We have chicken, pickles, cold biscuits and jam. And a custard pie . . ." She glanced at the small man. "Harold's favorite." She yawned again, covering the yawn with a small, kid-gloved hand.

The door at the far end of the car slammed open.

"Have some chicken, kid," the small man said, and nodded toward the open basket. "Take a piece, and give me one . . . and do it *now*."

Lee reached into the basket, found a piece of chicken wrapped in cheese cloth, and handed it over to the small man, Harold. Then, glancing down the length of the car, seeing four men standing there with rifles, while a smaller man—the marshal with the big mustache, he thought—stood talking to two men in rancher's clothes, sitting at the back. The huge Indian sat directly across, on the other side of the aisle. Could be there'd be trouble when they came to him.

"Take your chicken, boy," the small man said. "It's good," said the woman, and she pulled off her gloves, leaned over, reached in the basket and got a piece of chicken out and handed it to Lee. Then she reached in again, and brought out a biscuit with jam onit, and began to eat. She bit into it hungrily, and crumbs fell in her lap.

Lee took a bite of the chicken, though he was too scared to enjoy it, and found that he was wrong. It was fine roasted, and salted, and it tasted so good his jaw ached, chewing it. He had a breast, and the meat was thick, and rich.

If the lawmen called him—tried to put him under arrest—he'd have to go shooting. And go he certainly would. There were too many to put down.

Damn young to die, he thought. Oh, dear, I am too young to be shot dead.

"I sure wish we had some hard eggs," the small man said. "I'm that fond of a hard cooked egg. With mustard. That's prime!"

Lee saw that the lawmen had passed on beyond the big Indian. He must have managed to keep his crazy mouth shut, then, with those four rifles staring at him . . . ! Lee wished to God the giant had made a fuss—and pulled his pistol on the deputies, a hell of a shooting! Wished to God that had happened . . .

The lawmen were four seats away, peering through the dim light, water still dripping off their slickers. Lee could smell the rubbered canvas. They were poking a young man awake, the little marshal speaking to him mighty sharp.

"My name is Harold Duschied," the small man said to Lee, swallowing a bite of chicken. He'd had a leg, and was nearly finished with it. "This is my wife, Millie—maiden name McConnell, with two L's. You're her kid brother, Phil. Been working the winter in your dad's feed lot and slaughter, back in Fort Page. Mighty fed up with it, too, I'd say; glad enough to be visiting Millie and me in Portland." He winked, and a deputy stood in the aisle, looking down at them. A second deputy came up, a fat man with a hard fat face, and both of them glanced at the small man, looked longer at the woman, and then laid their eyes full on Lee, and kept them there.

Then didn't say anything, only stood and watched Lee as he chewed his bite of chicken.

"Say, boys," the small man, Duschied said, "what's the rub? Who're you hunting?"

One of the deputies, the fat one, glanced at him. "We're huntin' a kid just like this one. Shot a lawman in Grover, an' damn near killed him—did kill a drover!"

"Son-of-a-gun," Duschied said, "you hear that, Millie?" He grinned across at Lee. "Wild West, sure enough!" he said. And to the deputy, "Young Phil, here, he's been roughing it himself, working a feed lot all winter for his dad."

A wrinkled, knobby-knuckled hand came from between the deputies, and parted them. Its owner, the marshal, stepped in to look down at the three of them. He was an old man—almost elderly—with a Colt's Dragoon in a plain holster at his belt, and long, sweeping gray mustachios. His narrow face was carved deep in lines of age and weather, and he had eyes as red-rimmed, green, and savage as an old coyote's.

He bent a heavy gaze onto Lee. "What's your name, boy?" A light and pleasant voice, more youthful than the marshal's face. So close, his small size didn't seem to matter. He seemed larger than his deputies.

"McConnell. Phillip McConnell." Nervous, but not at all scared . . . that was the way. *God help me to it,* Lee thought.

"Your daddy's name—where's his feed lot at?" The marshal had been listening for a moment behind the curtain of his deputies' backs.

"Mister Jason McConnell, Esquire." Didn't know why he even said something so damn dumb! *Esquire!*

"Esquire . . . ?" The marshal's mouth appeared below his mustache. He thought that was pretty funny. His deputies must have felt that small smile, though they couldn't have seen it. They smiled, themselves.

"True enough," Duschied chimed in. "I married above myself, didn't I, Millie?"

"Yes," the woman said, and yawned. "I believe you did."

"Family's real rich," Duschied confided to the marshal, and he grinned. "But damned if I see any of it!"

The old marshal, like an elderly, fierce bird of prey, slowly turned his head and regarded Duschied. "This boy your wife's brother, then?"

"Kid brother and I suspect, a rip. Be pleased if you'd haul young Phil away, marshal. Be the best thing for him. Could sure use a tub bath, too, if you have one at the jail. Came aboard back at Fort Page smelling like a sick steer."

"I took a bath four days ago—with soap," Lee said, playing the sullen boy, and something short of sense.

"Must have been cow shit soap," Duschied said, and the deputies laughed.

The marshal didn't laugh. "You always go armed, boy?" he said to Lee, looking at the butt of the Remington poking out of his belt.

Lee played up as the snot. "I paid for it.—I guess I have a right to carry a pistol! Supposing somebody was to rob the train?"

The deputies thought that was funny, too. So did Duschied.

"Oh, you keep your mouth closed, Philly," the woman said, suddenly. "Don't be so smart!" This sudden remark, delivered in exactly the tone of an exasperated older sister, seemed to settle the matter for the marshal. He stared at Duschied and the woman for a moment, then at Lee for a moment more. Then he turned to his men.

"We'll take a look at the coaler an' engine," he said, "and check the bracing rods under the cars."

"Yes, marshal," the deputies said, and the three of them walked past the jakes, and out the car's door to do it.

"Rude old man," the woman said. "I need my medicine, Harold."

"Take it, my dear," said Duschied, and leaned over to pick out another piece of chicken for himself. He began to chuckle, and leaned back, taking a bite, then laughing a little more. A deputy, lingering behind, walked past them on his way after the marshal, and glanced curiously down at Duschied, which seemed to make him laugh the more. When he opened his mouth, laughing, Lee saw a wad of chewed chicken in there.

The woman had taken out her reticule and was fumbling in it. She found a tiny black bottle, twisted out the cork and, the first time Lee had seen anything of the sort done, except by children trying for a last drop of molasses—she stuck out her tongue, up-ended the bottle, and let just two drops of something milky fall. Then she licked her lips and swallowed.

Lee was reminded of the whore Mary Spots, and her tongue, and was embarrassed.

"Something for her nerves, kid," Duschied said, and tossed his chicken bone back into the basket. "You better have some more grub."

Lee thought he'd better, at that, and, thinking that the marshal might change his mind and come combing through again, soothed himself by digging out another breast of chicken, and a biscuit with jam in it. Proved to be strawberry jam.

When he'd swallowed the last of this biscuit—and not hearing by any noise of boots that the lawmen were coming back through—Lee thought it good time to ask the question.

"Mister Duschied—why did you put into this?"

The small man stared at him, not laughing, now. Then he said, over the gentle hubbub of the other passengers discussing all this fuss of deputies, and what it meant, and what desperado, and who, and never-heard-of-him, "Why, kid, I thought to do you a favor! Haven't I done you a favor?"

"Darn sure you have."

The small man smiled. "Then," he said, "you owe me one, in return."

"I suppose I do," Lee said. "And I'll do you any favor I can."

Duschied leaned forward and patted Lee on the knee. "I knew you were a right one," he said. "And, truth to tell, there is a small favor you might do us, kid. In Parker, we heard they'd be looking for a kid named Morgan. That your first name, or your last?"

"Lee Morgan's my name." Too late to play it cute with this fellow.

"Say," the woman said, seeming much more lively, "there go the coppers!" She was peering out the window, and suddenly pursed her lips into a kiss, and pressed them to the glass. "Goodbye," she called out, softly, and kissed the glass again.

"All right, Lee," Duschied said, with the air of a business man prepared to discuss affairs. At the same time, he leaned over, took the reticule from the woman's lap, opened it, took out the little bottle, and slipped that into the pocket of his suit.

"What in the world do you think you're doing?"

"You can have more, later, sweetie," Duschied said, handed her back her reticule, and leaned forward to talk to Lee. "You see, kid, Lee, we're robbing this train. And we had a third man, but we lost him in Parker . . ."

"Didn't we just," the woman said.

"So," the small man said, over the interruption, "you see our pickle. We need a third man to do the thing."

In a dream about this, Lee was sure he'd jump at such a chance. To rob a train! Considerable excitement, to be sure. Most boys had imagined something of that sort. Owl-hooting to a fare-thee-well! Now, however, with the memory of that old marshal's eye upon him, the memory of George Peach falling back, too, his face as stunned as a slapped child's . . .

Likely this fellow was japing, anyway.

"I guess I'd rather not," he said, and waited to see Duschied laugh. But Duschied shook his head seriously. "Of course you'd rather not!" he said. "What damn fool wouldn't rather not? I'd lots prefer to sit in a mansion on Beacon Hill in Boston, with a billiards table in a separate room, and a fine marble bar in another!" He frowned a peculiar frown, his brows drawn down, the ends of his mouth drawn down, too, like a little boy strikingly displeased. It was an almost funny face, he made, but not quite.

"But," he continued, still frowning, "I haven't the choice. And neither have you, kid, unless you have ten thousand dollars in gold, and don't need cash money, and never will!" His voice had risen during this, but not enough to be heard over the noise of the rain.

When he'd said that say, as if in punctuation, Lee heard the sharp *chuff* of the locomotive's gathering steam, and the car lurched slightly underneath him.

Duschied reached over and patted Lee on the knee again. Lee noticed that his hand, while not large at all, seemed thicker through than most, fat with muscle. He recalled the grip on his wrist, more like that a plumber's wrench might seize, than a man's hand and fingers.

"Doubt I'd be any good at it, either," he said, aware it wasn't the firmest reply. Truth was, Duschied could raise a hue and cry any time he chose. Lee was wanted, and no doubt about it; any talk of Duschied planning to rob a train, was just talk, and would be heard as a felon's angry stooling. "I've never been a robber."

"Oh, I believe you'll do, won't he, Millie?" Seemed that Millie was her real name, then, and not just a made-up for the marshal.

"Oh," she said, restlessly, shifting in the seat, "I'm sure of that, Harvey. Couldn't we get up and walk out on the car platform?"

"You called me 'Harvey,'" Duschied said to her, frowning, and he reached over and took her hand in both of his, pinched the long, polished nail of her forefinger between this thumb and first finger, and, with a quick, twisting wrench, tore it off.

The woman threw her head back in agony, her other hand over her mouth to stifle a scream, and then sat still, trembling, leaving her injured hand bleeding in Duschied's grip as though for comfort after the fact.

"Oh . . . my dear, you hurt me so," she said, faintly, gasping as if she were going to be sick. Her head thrown back under the soft glow of an oil lamp revealed eyelids, fluttered closed, so delicately blue-veined that they barely seemed to mask the glittering hazel beneath.

Duschied set the bleeding hand aside on the seat cushion before it could spot his suit. "Now, Millie—you know you were in the wrong." He glanced at Lee, and spoke softly, "She's a good split, and high-bred, too, her family's Presbyterian. But she's got a monkey, and gets careless sometimes." He paused a moment, and looked at the woman, who slowly opened her eyes, and began to sit up, biting her lip at the pain. "One'll grow back; you know that, Millie. Don't make such a fuss."

"I'm sorry . . . Harold," the woman said.

"I know you're a good girl," Duschied said, "but when you fly high, you get wordy. Now, you can't have any more, not for a while." He turned to Lee with a wink. "Can't do with 'em; can't do without 'em," he said. And then, "Now, listen to what we're going to do about earning some money—the easy way."

"I don't think I'd be much of a robber," Lee said. "I'd rather pass this hand, if you don't mind." He saw that Duschied still had the torn, bloody scrap of fingernail held between his thumb and forefinger.

Duschied frowned—and as he did, the railway car jolted, and began to slowly roll forward. Lee heard the engine laboring up ahead, through the noise of the rain-storm, and saw the lamp lit sheds of Carruthers slowly began to slide backward, into the night.

"Are you—" Duschied spoke softly, frowning like an angry child. "Are you trying to make me angry?" It was a query full of surprise, as though it was difficult for him to believe such a thing. He sat, holding the torn-off fingernail, waiting for Lee to answer him.

The woman sat silent beside the small man, her injured hand now held lightly in her lap, her small, white first finger capped with a bright but darkening bubble of blood.

Lee had had an exhausting day, and frightening. In an odd way, the dogs that had harassed him in the Parker shanties had seemed to wear him as much as anything. Then that damn crazy Indian taking an offence at nothing, then the deputies—and now this. Lee was young, and he was tired, and—truth to tell—he was scared of Duschied. The small man, with no weapon showing, except those powerful square hands, had an air about him—as well as a considerable smell of lavender water—of dangerous force. Not simply by the nasty trick he'd done with the woman, but more, by a sort of unworried quality he had. He hadn't seemed to be concerned about the marshal and his deputies at all.

Wasn't concerned about Lee's Remington at all, either—nor the fact he'd just shot a couple of men with it.

It wasn't natural. It was frightening, was what it was. It seemed to Lee that he had fallen into some nightmare—starting with his killing George. A nightmare where each passage dreamed, got worse and worse. Well, he was tired, and he was scared, and he wanted to wake up.

"Are you against me?" Duschied asked, with the same puzzled incredulity, still frowning that strange, dark frown.

"No," Lee said. "I'm not against you." Truth was, he'd run out of sand. He'd had the feeling—more than the feeling—that his string was about to run out with Mister Duschied. And Remington or not, gun speed or not, he'd just decided not to see what Mister Duschied would do about it. It was shaming and relieving at once to see Duschied's frown instantly clear from his face. The small, natty fellow sat back in his seat, pleased and satisfied.

"There now," he said, "I almost misunderstood you." He motioned to the picnic basket. "I know you kids. You're always hungry. Go on, bring out that custard pie, and we'll have a slice. There's some fine sweet peach brandy in there, too, if you'd care for a nip?"

"I guess not," Lee said, and though he'd rather have slept than have more food—Duschied had about spoiled his appetite—he dug into the basket, found the pie, already cut in half and wrapped in napkins, and handed one of the halves to Duschied.

"O.K.!" Duschied liked the look of the pie. And, without Lee seeing where he got it, he had a large jackknife open in his hand, and was neatly slicing the half in half again, not dropping a crumb. Lee saw that he had gotten rid of the woman's fingernail. Duschied handed Lee his piece of the pie—nicely baked. A golden-brown filling, just solid enough and dusted with cinnamon, a fine, thin, flaky crust.

It was delicious.

"Millie," Duschied said, "it's damn near as good as yours."

"Thank you, Harold," she said, and kept her eyes closed.

"Now," Duschied said, his mouth full of pie for Lee to see, "this is what we intend." He swallowed, and bit off another bite. "We intend," he said, thickly, "to go on back to the express car—which is behind the last two passenger cars—get them to open up (they'll have no choice on that because we'll have the conductor, and the passengers) and, once the car is open, to open the strong box." He swallowed. "There's thirty-one thousand dollars in gold in that strong box." He took the last bite of his pie. And while chewing, "One o'clock in the morning, we're going to do that. While everyone's dopey—" He grinned over at the woman. "No offense, sweetie."

A bite of pie seemed to stick in Lee's throat. "There's a lot of people on this train," he said, keeping his voice down. "A lot of armed men . . ."

Duschied seemed surprised and amused. "You are a caution, kid," he said. "Armed men!" He chuckled, licking a crumb from his lower lip. "Lots of fellows carry weapons, kid. That don't mean they got the sand to use them or the know-how to, either!" He turned a little sideways in his seat, and neatly crossed his legs, so that one shiny black shoe rested near Lee's right knee. "I suppose that me and Moon—and you—can handle any nosey Parkers." He smiled, and shook his head. "Armed men," he said, and smiled, and shook his head. "You hear that?" he said to the woman, but she didn't answer.

"I bet that finger hurts like sixty," Duschied said to Lee. There was nothing much Lee could think of to reply. And it damn sure looked like he was going to be a train robber, like it or not. Duschied, this Mister Moon, and him. Lord only knew what the woman, Millie, was supposed to do while they were robbing the train.

Duschied yawned.

"You can please yourself," he said. "Was I you, kid, I'd get me some sleep. Not many hours to go, and then the job, and then we jump for our horses and ride for a few days." He tilted his head back on the seat rest. "Were I you, I'd get some shut-eye." And, with that, shut his eyes, and, in a minute or two, seemed to have fallen dead asleep, the Macassar oil in his neatly combed hair shining in the lamplight.

Lee considered getting slowly up—not just yet, but in awhile—as if he were going for a piss. Then—a step out onto the car platform—and a harder, darker, wetter, steeper step out into the night and off the train, however fast it might be going.

He sat, shifting slightly to the motions of the train, watching the two people sitting opposite. Both asleep, it seemed. The rain had let up, outside, but still some tail end of the storm buffeted the car, wind gusts hummed past the windows, shook the hurtling steel faintly from side to side.

Most of the passengers were asleep now, the excitement of the searching deputies all past and talked over and talked out. Lee looked down the car's length to see the huge Indian, and could barely make out the man's bulk in the gloom. A man and wife slept together one row of seats down and across the aisle. They leaned into each other, sleeping, the man's hat brim shading his eyes, the feathers stuck in the woman's hat slowly nodding to the rhythm of her breaths. Lee could see a child's foot—their child, asleep in the seat reversed to face them. It was a little girl. Lee could see the small white-stockinged ankle, the shiny little patent leather high button boot.

Duschied certainly seemed deeply asleep, he drew harsh, regular breaths, his head now turned sideways on the seat-back, showing more of the curve of white, spotless collar.

Lee was thinking of getting up . . . of going to make that jump. It would mean leaving his possibles —and, right now, he didn't mind that at all. He could always earn more goods—walk 'till morning, 'till he came to a farm or ranch. Chore his way. He'd done it before, and wasn't afraid of the work.

He thought of his father for a moment—had the odd notion he'd be pleased to see the old man—

nearly an old man, anyway—come limping down the car aisle right now. Though he wouldn't be able to do damn-all, anymore. Though Lee wanted no part of him, in any case . . .

Not yet. No move yet. Wait a few minutes more. Perhaps an hour more. Then, up to the jakes—and out and gone. Be a relief to leave the damn dude Indian behind, as well. Be a hell of a relief to leave the whole damn train behind! Been nothing but deep manure, since he'd caught on to it and been boarded by those Texicans.

Not yet. But in a while . . .

And just when he was thinking that, the woman, Millie, opened her eyes and looked at him. She had beautiful eyes, like an actress's or an opera dancer's. She stared right at him, as if she was reading his mind, and then, very very slowly, shook her head once, from side to side.

It said: *I know—and don't try it.* And it scared Lee more than he'd been scared before, but not as much as Duschied's voice, as he seemed to sleep deep as a lake, eyes closed, head cosy against the seat back.

"Good advice," said Mister Duschied.

Lee woke with a start. No reason. No one had spoken, or touched him. He'd slept deep, dreamed deep, too. One of those generous, involving dreams that seemed as rich as life itself. He'd been on Spade Bit, working horses. Mrs. Dowd had been out by the corral fence, watching Lee and George Peach work a colt called "Bobwire." The colt, a nice stepping black, had thrown Lee hard, after a hard ride. Though in the dream, the jolts and switching, bucking and sun-fishing, had seemed slower, easier to ride with. None the less, though slowly and easily, Lee had parted company, and dived down into the dirt right on his hat. "Well ridden, anyway!" Mrs. Dowd had called to him. But George had just laughed. "If you could ride as good as you shoot," George had said, standing laughing in his fancy pinto-hide chaps, "you wouldn't be down in that dirt. Don't you mind what a lady says," he went on, "I'm shot dead, and I should know what I'm talkin' about!"

Then—while he was getting up from the corral dirt—Lee woke up to the motion of the train, the dull, repeating thud and clack of the wheels underneath him.

It was the middle of the night—deep in the night; he could smell the hot oil in the little lamps below the luggage racks.

Duschied and the woman were awake and looking at him.

"Kid," Duschied said softly, as if not to wake any of the people sleeping around them, "you sleep like a hound dog—damn if you don't! Did you see that, Millie! Boy's legs were twitchin' like a pup's." The small man leaned forward. "Ready to go robbing, boy?" Lee saw that he had a gold-cased watch in his hand. "It's time."

In the deep manure, and no spade handy. Maybe there'd be a chance, later, for a break.

"Yes," Lee said. "I am."

"Then bring your goods but forget that saddle back there," Duschied said, reached under his seat, pulled out a small canvas bag, then stood up, beckoned to Lee with his head, and started down the aisle toward the back of the train. Lee stood, shouldered his sack, and followed Duschied down. He glanced back, and saw that the woman was coming after them. She had a small leather personals case in her right hand; she held her injured hand out, away from her skirts as she walked. She was tall, and looked slender. As tall as Duschied, or almost. As Lee followed the man down the aisle, he figured Duschied at five foot, nine—nor much more. Maybe a hundred and sixty pounds. A small man. He didn't look like much from the back, only particularly neat, wearing good clothes.

Lee wondered if he wasn't showing a great deal of yellow, just going along with the man, like this, because he'd played tough, and hurt a woman. But yellow or not, he was damn sure going along.

Duschied got to the end of the car, turned, and waited for Lee and the woman to catch up. He seemed as easy as if they were going to a fancy dining car for a late supper.

Lee glanced to the right at the end of the car, looking to see if the big Indian was awake. He was—and looking back at Lee. There was no expression on his face at all. Lee could see the gleaming black of his eyes in the shadow of the brim of that fine gray plug hat. That had to be a big city bought hat, from Chicago, maybe.

Ahead of him, Duschied pulled the car door open, and stepped through, onto the platform. Lee, and then the woman, went after him.

The storm was over, but its mark was still on the sky. A half moon shone shifting through streams of clouds as the train rattled along. The wind of passage was icy chill. It would be cold riding, later—if there was a later. It occurred to Lee that once he'd helped Duschied with his robbery—and the fellow Moon—there wouldn't be much reason for them to keep him alive to claim a share. It would do, he thought, to be ready to use the Remington, however Duschied daunted him.

Duschied had started to pull the door to the next car open, when Lee, glancing back, saw they had company. Looming above the woman, Millie, though walking behind her, the Indian giant stalked after them, swaying for balance on the shaking platform.

Lee reached out, and caught Duschied's coat sleeve. "There's a man following us. I've had trouble with him."

Duschied turned his head, saw the Indian behind them, and grinned at Lee. "Picked a bone with you, did he? Well, don't be too concerned. He does that with most. He won't trouble you while you're with us."

"He's—?"

"That's Mister Moon. Mister Broken Moon, that is." And Duschied turned, pulled the car door full open, and started away from the aisle.

Lee glanced back at the Indian—saw him standing patiently, looming above Duschied's woman like a storm cloud, gray suit, half lit by moonlight—and turned to follow Duschied down the passenger car aisle.

A nightmare, for sure.

He passed the fat woman and her fat little boy, both asleep, looked up, and saw the conductor stepping into the car at the far end. Duschied broke into a near trot, heading down the aisle toward the man, and Lee—and, he supposed, the other two odd companions—followed after.

Duschied had met the conductor alongside the first row of seats, almost at the end of the car, and Lee hurried past a snoring thin fellow, half spilled out into the passageway aisle, and dead asleep, and caught up to the small man.

The conductor seemed sleepy, and confused. "What . . . ?" he was saying to Duschied. "What did you say?" He was keeping his voice down, and Duschied did likewise.

"I was introducing my young friend, here," he said, "the Idaho Kid." He winked at Lee. "We intend to rob your train."

The conductor woke up at that, opened his mouth —and stood silent as a stone.

Lee hadn't seen where it came from; he assumed that Duschied had had it held in his hand down at his side . . . just held it out of sight. But now, the small man had put the muzzle of a short barreled revolver to the conductor's throat. It was a Colt's forty-five Sheriff's Model.

And must have felt like death to the conductor.

Duschied kept talking to the man in that same soft voice. "I don't," he said, "want to disturb these folks by putting a hole in that ugly red mark you have there." The pistol muzzle was pressed against the red birthmark on the man's throat. "But that sure is a foul-looking thing," Duschied said. "Bet no woman can bear to look at that! That's almost as bad looking as one of those big lumpy things with hair growing out of it. Any hair grow out of this thing?

"Well?" he was almost whispering. He pushed the

blunt muzzle of the revolver deeper into the man's neck.

"No," the conductor said. There were tears in his eyes, whether from fear, or pain from the revolver muzzle, Lee couldn't tell.

"No what?"

"No . . . no hair . . ."

Duschied, looking pleased, turned his head to whisper to Lee and the woman and Indian following, "He doesn't have any hair growing out of this mark . . ."

Lee looked up and down the dark aisle, trying to see if any person who was not a crazy man, or a drugged girl, or a great thug of a savage Indian might be awake, might be seeing what was happening, drawing a pistol to put a stop to it.

Right there, right in front of a whole railroad car full of sleeping people, Duschied then reached down with his free hand and suddenly gripped at the conductor's privates.

The man jumped back with an exclamation—but a muffled one, a sort of very soft shout, as if he, too, agreeing with Duschied, was determined to wake none of the sleepers.

Duschied turned to wink at the woman. "Hasn't got much, Millie. Nothing there for a real full-blooded woman." Then without pausing, he began to push the conductor back toward the car door and platform beyond it. "Git . . . git . . . git!" As if the poor man—tears on his cheeks, now—were some varmint steer, wandered into a cabbage patch.

Lee could see the man's terrified eyes, rolling like a darky's, as Duschied pushed him back out of the car. The conductor was being very quietly chivvied out of the sleeping company and lamp light and back into the dark. It seemed, now, to mean a great deal to him. He seemed to think he would be killed.

Lee thought so, too.

Still making no noise but that almost whispered "git . . . git . . . go on, now . . ." Duschied backed the man to the car door, reached around his passive body to grip the handle, pushed it open, and gently shoved the weeping man back and through, into the night.

"Cain't you make up yore mind, Charlie?"

The Texicans. Leaning on the left side rail of the platform.

Lee assumed they must have quit their drinking to come in during the hours of storm. But if they had, and perhaps caught some sleep, they were now back where they had been when they'd hauled him aboard. Still, or again, quite drunk. Still big, still dangerous, still armed.

All hell appeared to be about to pop. Lee took a long step to the right side, until that platform rail struck his back, and drew the Remington—though in some doubt who he'd be shooting at.

The conductor—in the jaws of the serpent—had said nothing to the tall drover's pleasantry. Both the Texans were leaning against the platform's opposite rail, slickered and mufflered against the cold night air, their broad brim hats pulled down to their ears. The tall one had a jar of something clear as water in his hand.

Duschied shoved the conductor on ahead of him, and, the short barreled revolver plain in the moonlight, said, cheerfully, "We're robbing the train, boys —wish us luck!" And appeared to take no more heed of the two drovers than that.

"I'll be go to hell! Damn if it don't look like you ain't!" the tall drover said. "Shit," the short one said, peering through the uncertain moonlight. "Ain't they got a gun on old Charlie?" He sounded very drunk.

"They're robbin' the train, you damn fool," the tall one said.

"Come on, Idaho," Duschied called to Lee as the woman and Indian filed over the platform.

"Look at the fuckin' size on that red nigger?" the short drover said, as the Indian walked past him. The Indian paid him no heed.

Lee followed the giant along. Didn't appear that the drovers were going to save his butt twice.

"All right, now, boys," the tall drover called after them, as Duschied shoved the conductor—the man was whimpering, trying to say something—through the doorway into the next car.

"It ain't none of our put-in. But don't you go shootin' Charlie!"

"Don't you hurt that lady, neither," the other one shouted. Lee wondered if that had wakened anyone. The express people, anyway.

The Indian turned and pulled the express car door shut behind them, and Lee found himself crowded in a narrow vestibule, the woman, a soft, rustling pressure of attar-of-roses, whalebone strips, and flesh softness—the Indian, who seemed to pay Lee no mind at all, now—pressing against his other side like a brick wall.

There was an odor of human shit. The conductor, who, it appeared, had emptied his bowels, was crying, and murmuring something to Duschied.

"I know," Duschied said to him. "I know just what you mean . . ."

He and the conductor, lit by the vestibule's one oil lamp, stood together, facing a narrow door. The door was oak planking, bound with iron bands. There was a tiny spy-door, three or four inches square, let into it high in the center.

"Give them the secret knock, Charlie," Duschied said to the conductor, having apparently picked up the name when the drover had called it.

"Those Texicans are going to wake the train," Lee said. Seemed that someone should say it!

"Oh, perhaps," Duschied said, turning his head to look at Lee. He smiled. "Say, kid," he said, "I noticed that nifty draw you worked out there. Not *too* slow . . ." He winked again, a small, well-dressed man without a care in the world, then turned back to the narrow door, and said, "Wake 'em up, Charlie."

Blinking, his cheeks shining with tears in the lamplight, the conductor knocked softly on the oak planks. He knocked once—then three times fast.

The drover's shouting had wakened someone, after all.

The little door in the big door's center suddenly clicked and snapped back, and part of a young man's face, and all of a hard brown eye appeared in that opening.

"Trouble?" The word came snapping through the little window as if sounded by a soldier.

"Oh . . . oh, Bob," the conductor managed, his voice shaking, and, as abruptly as it had opened, the little window snapped shut.

"Rude," Duschied said, and appeared to think for a moment. He knocked on the door panels himself, hitting the door hard with his fist.

"Listen to me, in there!" he said. "This is a robbery

and it's the cash money that we want. We don't wish to injure a soul! And we won't do so, either, if you will accomodate us . . ."

He struck the door with his fist again.

"Don't force us to injure this fellow now, he's done no harm to deserve that. I say, don't force us to it!"

Duschied stood quiet for a moment, listening, and Lee could hear men talking through the door's heavy planking.

"Open the door to us now and there'll be no violence," Duschied said, and listened again.

No sound at all on the other side of the door.

"You are cruel and thoughtless men," Duschied said, "and you leave us no choice."

Then he turned to the conductor, and Lee saw with some surprise that he no longer had the revolver in his hand. The large jackknife was there instead, and open.

Far ahead, the train's engine seemed to redouble its effort. Lee could hear the hoarse, roaring coughs as the crew raised more steam, opened the throttle wider. There was a slant to the flooring beneath them now; they were climbing a grade.

"I'm going to take care of that thing there for you," Duschied said to the conductor. "You'll look better with it gone." And leaped up and onto the man like a cat of great size, dressed in a fine dark suit.

The conductor screamed and tried to strike at him, batting at him with his fists in a flurry. Duschied paid no heed. He balanced himself up on the man like a circus acrobat, and gripping his face with one terrible hand, forced his head back, and began cutting his throat.

He looked to be slicing into the man's birthmark,

his elbow wagging as he worked the knife—and the conductor was down on the express car floor, shrieking like a woman, and blood in quick warm blurts came spattering at them in the narrow space.

It struck the side of Lee's face, and he saw some on the woman's dress, bright as paint in the lamplight. A spray of droplets of it was dotted on the wall in front of them and drops running down the narrow oak panels of the door.

The Indian stood against him half asleep, or so he seemed, taking no notice of the terrific noise, the high-pitched squeals the man was making.

Lee saw the woman, her lips pursed, dig into her reticule and take a Derringer pistol out. More blood had sprayed on the sleeve of her dress.

Lee heard shouts behind the locked oak door.

And, as if there'd been a signal, the screaming stopped.

Instead, a slow, deep, gargling sound. A bubbling sound, like a cellar spring running underneath a house floor. And with this, a rapid tripping tapping noise.

Lee, who hadn't looked after the conductor had fallen, after seeing the strenuous motions of Duschied's arm, looked now.

Duschied was up, frowning. His right hand was empty, the jackknife magically gone again. He held a wet small patch in his other hand, that might have been red before it was bloodied.

At his feet, kicking in a small regular way, his heels drumming on the car's steel flooring, the conductor was drowning in his own blood, gargling it deep into his lungs with every heaving attempted breath.

Duschied examined the patch for a moment, then

flicked it away. His suit was spoiled with blood. "If this fool had just held still," he said. "I'd have got it off and no harm done. But he would shake this way and that . . ."

Duschied stepped past the trotting feet—trotting more slowly, now, as the conductor began to die—and struck the narrow door again, hitting it hard with his fist.

"You have made me do a murder!" he called through the iron-bound door, and hit it with his fist again. "Don't make me to another! We have a young lady here, a passenger. A most genteel young lady . . ."

There were loud voices behind the door, a shout—and silence.

"Would you sacrifice a lady . . . a lovely lady . . . for the Company's gold?"

Lee had heard a stage actor acting in the Silver Theatre in Butte. The fellow had declaimed much as Duschied; a sort of ranting, it was—from Shakespeare, then, from true life, now.

The floor was slippery under his boots. Beside him, Millie cocked her little Derringer, and stepped across the vestibule to the oak door, and pressed up against it, so that her face was by the little spy window.

Duschied stood to one side, to give her room. The conductor's shoes lay finally still beside her small high button boots.

Beyond the car door, out on the platform, Lee heard a man cursing, boots ringing on the steel flooring. Lee thought that if such a nightmare got deeper, got deep enough, then it would surely get down to death, itself. The woman, Duschied, the huge Indian hulking here beside him—all of them seemed as flat as painted pictures—seemed hardly to move . . .

The woman's mouth opened, her white teeth shining in the lamplight.

"Ohhh, please! Oh, please don't. My children . . . my babies!" Her voice had an odd rolling, rising note to it, a mad rocking up and down as she cried out. She'd heard a woman cry out like that . . . cry those things, Lee thought. Some other woman in Duschied's hands, while Millie was there . . . watched . . .

"*Ohhh—don't do that! DON'T DO THAT!!*" And she screamed. Lee had never heard a sound like it in his life.

A shout from behind the narrow door—the clack and whack of a long bolt snapping back—and the door was swung open as quickly as if it had been tissue deal, and not iron-bound oak.

A young man with a shotgun came out of the door. Tall, thin, in his shirt sleeves. Brown eyes and going bald, although young. He came out fast, looking in a rage, rather than frightened. Saw the woman in front of him—tried to bring the shotgun to bear—and the long double-barrel struck the side of the door and delayed him only for the slightest fraction of a second. He must have chosen the shotgun as the most fearsome weapon—its murderous, gaping muzzles—and forgotten its unhandyness in such close quarters.

Lee saw that in one sudden seeing—and heard the first shot that Millie fired into the young fellow—saw the haze of smoke rise from between them.

Hit hard and dying, the young man staggered back into his strong room. He had forgotten the shotgun entirely in his surprise at Millie, and what she had just done to him.

The woman shot him a second time, and the young man fell to one knee, as if he'd slipped. Past the woman's shoulder, Lee could see a black hole in the man's white shirt. The burning powder must have made that when the bullet thumped into him.

The young man fell over sideways as Duschied shoved past Millie and went into the room. Lee thought he might have killed both of them right then, and then decided not to do it. He looked to his side to see what the Indian intended, and as he did, the car door to the platform crashed open, and the tall Texican drover came in shooting right hand and left.

The blasting noise seemed to push Lee down to the floor. He felt the slugs cracking over his head, and rolled up on his elbow to kill the drover before the man killed him.

A louder noise came then. It deafened Lee and sent a spike of pain through both ears. He saw the Indian, big as a mountain, standing, almost toe to toe, with the drover—and in one huge red fist, the giant Walker's Colt looked big as an anvil. It went off again—silently for Lee—and the tall driver vanished, folded away and fell back through a cloud of gunsmoke.

As that man fell away, Lee saw a lick of flame from past the doorway, and the Indian flinched, and shifted a foot. The second Texican, his round face red with rage, had gotten a field of fire clear, with his friend's death, and used it, firing again.

Lee heard him yell something about "a lady" and his third shot burned the skin off Lee's arm under the elbow. Then the drover leveled for a fourth.

The big Indian fired and missed, and Lee was deaf

again. He shot through the smoke and hit the Texan in the face, on the left side, above the man's cheek. The Texan was wrenched out from behind the frame of the car door, staggered across the platform—triggering a shot into the steel flooring as he went—and the Indian fired again, struck the drover in the stomach, and killed him.

Lee felt wide awake now. He had no more slows. He felt pretty good, in fact, felt as though he could move quicker than any man alive. He was sorry about the Texican. Man had helped him on the train . . . but had no business firing at him; that was all there was to it. He supposed a decent man would call him a dirty dog for it, just the same.

His ears were buzzing from the gunfire; the little vestibule was full of smoke. A gunshot cracked outside, from the platform. Some other passengers come out, now, to take a hand.

Lee couldn't tell where the bullet went.

Then a second one, which went past his head and into a wall of the car. He swung up at the small oil lamp with the barrel of the Remington, smashed the glass, and put out that light. Lucky; might well have set the damn car on fire . . .

Another shot from out on the platform.

The Indian fired back—the crash of the Walker ringing off railroad steel.

There was still lamplight in the strong room. Lee walked in in a draft of gunsmoke. Under his boots—sticking slightly to the floor was he walked—he felt the train still shuddering up the grade.

All of this had taken not much time.

Duschied was talking to two men, down at the end of a long counter. Millie leaned against it, watching.

"Come on down, Kid," Duschied called, and beckoned Lee on. "Sounds like you an' Moon have had some business out there . . ." The "business," which still sounded in an occasional gunshot—an occasional cannon-like reply—didn't appear to trouble him, or give him cause to hurry.

"Go on with what you were saying, Mick," he said to a short man with dashing Burnsides and a red, boozer's nose. "It is 'Mick,' isn't it?"

"Yes, sir," the man with the Burnsides said. "But I can't open that safe. I just can't." This fellow's hands were shaking, and he put them palm down on the counter, to hold them still.

"Can't—or won't?" Duschied said, in a friendly way.

"Bob Trask was the only one had the combination. I swear that!"

"Do you?" Duschied said, and began to frown.

It occurred to Lee that Duschied's lady might have cost him considerable, killing young Mister Trask—for that was who the fellow with two forty-four shots in his chest appeared to have been. Should never have come out with that long gun—of course, should never have come out at all . . .

"Oh, for God's sake, for the love of God, Mick, open the god-damned safe!" said the other expressman, his face as white as bleached cotton. He was an older man, short and stocky, with one bright blue eye—his left—and the other covered with a small leather patch that tied around the back of his head with a string. This man looked to have been sorting mail when the trouble had started, for he still gripped a crumpled bunch of letters in his right hand.

Mick—who'd thus been proved mighty brave, or stupid—cut a frightened glance at his work-mate. "You know I don't have the combination, Hector." Brave, or stupid.

Lee thought, in dealing with Duschied and his two friends—he didn't count himself among them, dead drover or not—that brave or stupid tended to amount to the same thing.

Duschied was frowning deeply now, looking very disappointed in the expressman.

There was a crack of rifle fire outside—the snap and bang as bullets struck into the car's vestibule. A pause. Then the thunderous report of the Walker Colt.

"Old Moon . . . " Duschied said, but still bent his frown on the expressman. "I do hate a liar," he said. "I do despise a man who'll tell a lie."

"Mick—Mick, you damn fool! Open the god-damned safe for these people!" Old One-eye was terrified, and Lee was sorry he had come in here to see what Duschied would do now. *"Don't you know?"* the old man said. *"You God-damned fool—it's Harvey Logan! It's Kid Curry you're talkin' to!"*

Lee stared, as stock still as the expressman, and felt a slow pressure of ice along his spine. *Harvey Logan.* The last, and most murderous of the Wild Bunch. Cassidy . . . Sundance Kid . . . The Tall Texan . . . all jailed or run to South America. And even Harry Tracy, that mad dog, had walked quiet around this small, neatly dressed fellow, who looked like an officer in a bank.

Kid Curry. Broke out of a Tennessee jail, last Lee had heard stories about him . . . noosed a deputy with wire unwoven from a broom to do it . . .

And now, as Lee watched him, Mister Duschied's frown deepened into something more extreme, until his face hardly seemed a human face at all.

His voice, though, hadn't changed. "Silly fellows," he said.

The gunshot made Lee jump. He thought he'd seen a draw, but wasn't sure. Logan had the Sheriff's Model out, and it was smoking at the muzzle.

The old one-eyed man bent backward at the waist—as though showing how limber he could be despite his years. The top of his head was gone, and his brains—red scrambled eggs—tipped out as his head went back, and struck the floor before he did.

Logan stood at ease, his face fully human again, amused, and he negligently waved the revolver at the expressman with Burnsides.

"Open the safe, Mick," he said.

"I will . . . I will," the expressman said, and hurried across the car to do it. The woman, Millie, stood watching.

Lee thought that Logan might kill him next. And he didn't see any way to prevent it. He had the Remington still out and in his hand, and he knew he was quicker than most with a pistol, but he was no fool. He had never seen any man as fast with a revolver as Logan was. And he'd never seen any man surer than Logan was, either.

If he tried a shot, then Logan would certainly kill him. It was that simple. Kid Curry was way up out of Lee's class—for now, at any rate. And now is what counted.

"Relax, Idaho," Logan said, and smiled at him. Then looked over his shoulder at the expressman laboring over the safe. "Hurry that up, there!"

Bent over the safe, fumbling at the combination, the expressman said something.

"What?" Logan said.

"Are you going to shoot me? Are you going to shoot me . . . ?" the man said, his head bowed over his work, not trying to look up. "I swear . . . I swear to my dear God . . . I swear to my mother's soul that I will never tell . . ." He'd said all that he could say. His mouth was drawn down as if he were crying.

"Oh, get that safe open, you cry baby!" Logan said. "I will likely shoot you—and why shouldn't I? Whose fault is it that you refused what I asked, that your friend spilled a secret I want kept?" He tapped his fingers impatiently on the sorting counter. There was a volley of shots outside, then, that made Lee jump. It seemed to him that Kid Curry or not, time was running out.

"It's open . . . it's open, Mister . . ." The expressman crawled away from the open safe door. Either he couldn't stand up, or didn't want to . . . hoped that Logan would not shoot him if he were sitting down with his head turned away.

Logan took up a mail sack from the end of the counter, and handed it to Lee. "Load it up," he said, "and fast." He looked down at the expressman. "Millie," he said, still staring at the man, "go out and help Moon. We'll be there presently."

"I don't know who you are," the expressman said, talking like a child, in a child's high soft voice. "I don't know who you are . . ."

There were a dozen and more small weighty sacks of gold in the express company safe, those, and bundles of papers, and envelopes with yellow printing on them. Lee packed the heavy, small sacks into the canvas mailbag. He wished the expressman would stop talking.

The shot made his ears ring. It seemed louder than any shot. Louder even than the Indian's huge revolver firing.

He finished packing the mailbag, stood up, and followed Logan's neatly suited back, as he walked out of the express car. He didn't look back at the expressman with Burnsides, to see how he'd been placed beyond fearing anything.

The smoke-filled vestibule trembled to a thunder of gunfire.

Logan, crouching at the strong room door, beckoned Lee to him, shouting to be heard over the noise. "We have to have this platform out there clear of shooting! Our horses are waiting at the top of the grade. We have to be out there to get 'em!"

Clear enough. Lee was worried this crazy man was going to order him out there, shooting. It sounded as though four or five men, passengers with rifles and revolvers, were shooting into the express car from across that platform. Glancing out fast, Lee saw a flash and then another, as people fired from the open doorway of the passenger car.

He put his head out again, even quicker, and saw the Indian and Millie, both stretched out flat on their bellies on the vestibule floor, returning the storm of fire, the blast of the Walker Colt, mingling with the slight snapping sound of the woman's Derringer. Only the train's irregular jolting had kept them alive this long, and both had blood on them—but whether from the slaughtered conductor or their own wounds, Lee couldn't tell.

"I'll be going out to clear that platform," Logan

said to him, talking loud in Lee's ear to make himself heard. "You fire with the others to keep it clear, once I'm over the rail after the horses." He reached up and tapped Lee sharply on the shoulder. As he did, a rifle round came buzzing by them and splintered a chunk from the strong room door frame. "You take care of the cash," he said in Lee's ear. "You understand me?"

Lee nodded that he did.

Then Logan jumped back into the strong room, bent over the first of the dead men there—Bob, had been his name—grasped hold of the corpse, lifted it, and heaved it up half over his shoulder. Balancing nicely, Harvey Logan then ran back past Lee with that lolling burden running blood down his fine suit trouser leg, trotted straight out onto the open platform and into a blaze of gunfire.

Lee heard and felt that storm of lead come past him where he crouched by the express car door. Millie and the Indian, Moon, both bowed their heads to that concentrated fire, and hugged the steel plating underneath them.

Lee risked his life just to lean out to look—but he could no more have helped doing it, than breathing. And it was worth it, for he saw a sight most men wouldn't care to even dream of.

Mister Harvey Logan—Kid Curry, to the Eastern newspapers—stood braced wide-legged in the moonlight, weighted and shielded by a corpse (and staggering, even so, as bullets thudded into the dead man) and, as the train groaned underneath them all, slowing and slowing on the steepening grade, lifted a short-barreled revolver, and fired five, slow, deliberate shots into the gunflashes not twelve feet from where he stood.

Lee heard the corpse grunting as the lead smashed into it, save the five slow, slow spaced shots. Heard a man scream at the second. Men shouting at the fourth and fifth. And saw motion—a scrambling kind of motion, where Logan had shot into the open door, down the aisle of the passenger car.

No gun flashes followed those five aimed shots—not for a long moment.

And Logan was gone. The expressman's corpse flung down, and Logan leaped to the side of the platform, over the rail, and gone.

Then, someone in the passenger car fired again.

Lee shot back twice—jumped up and into the vestibule, and back into a haze of gunsmoke—past the Indian and Millie as they got to their feet—bent, and found his possibles sack in a wide slick of blood from the throat-cut conductor. Lugging that, and the mailbag weighted with gold, Lee followed Moon and the woman out onto the platform.

Someone fired at them from the passenger car door again—had to be at least one mighty hard case in there, to be sticking this firm in such a shooting—and Moon fired back, the muzzle-flash of the Walker Colt lighting the smoke haze as they made it to the platform rail.

Lee tripped, and went down to one knee as that hard case fired another shot at them—a rifle, it sounded like—and found he'd stepped over one of the dead Texicans. The short one, it seemed to be; he could make out a ruined face in the moonlight.

Horses.

A noise of running horses. Lee heard them off to the right, heard a man shouting. Answering shouts from inside the passenger car. Some people in there didn't want to let them off.

"God help us," Lee said to nobody, "those folks will hang us right here, if they catch us!" And so they would. A god-damned massacre, was what it had been!

A man on horseback came riding right up beside the slowing train—up alongside the right side of the platform. Lee looked for it to be Logan—wished it to be. Deep in hell, a devil was what suited.

It wasn't Logan; it was a tall young man with a skimpy chin beard—some red or yellow color, Lee thought, seeing it by moonlight.

Then, tired and ready for it in some way, Lee was shot at and hit.

One more of those rifle shots came popping—and kicked him alongside his left ribs, and knocked him down.

Lee dropped his possibles, pulled the Remington, and fired back. He didn't know if he was killed or not, but the blow had been shocking, worse than he had imagined being shot might feel.

He lay on the steel flooring, feeling the night air, chill as iced water, blowing in his face. His left arm felt as if it were asleep.

The Remington was in his right hand. He tried to cock it for another shot. It seemed that fellow with the rifle in there had gone too far, to keep shooting this way. There had been enough shooting, he thought.

Galloping horses, and pistol shots right beside him. He thought he heard Logan calling, "Millieee . . . Millieeee . . .!"

Something was at him like a bear, and Lee roused

and tried for a shot. The damn animals would scavenge a wounded man, he'd heard . . .

He felt the revolver knocked aside, felt himself lifted up like a baby . . .

That's all right, he thought. That doesn't hurt me . . .

He woke, riding.

Tried to sit up—and felt terribly sick. The worst he'd ever felt. He leaned off to the side of the horse's withers, retched—and then vomited a belly full.

Chicken . . . ?

Some damned stuff.

Dark. It was dark as pitch. And the horse wouldn't be still. It was going and going at a gallop, and him with no hand at all on the reins . . .

Lee's left side hurt like sixty, and he couldn't recall why. May have had a fall. Dark night, but he looked around, spit some mess out of his mouth, and saw horsemen around him on either side. All riding like the devil to somewhere!

He tried to say something, to call out, but his mouth was too dry after that vomiting. His feet felt strange in the stirrups, and when he tried to shift them, he couldn't. He reached down with his right hand to find out why, and felt some rope tied in a knot down there.

He was tied in the saddle.

As he rode, the wind made him feel better, more and more awake. But the more he woke up, the more his left side hurt him. Damned if he wouldn't like to cut the whole thing off and leave it—just throw all that side away. That would have to feel better, doing that, than just galloping along in the damned dark with it hurting like this.

Cut it off the way Logan had cut that poor old conductor's birthmark off . . .

Lee remembered everything, then, and would have given anything he was ever going to get to be somewhere else right now. To be a different person entirely, and have his mother there. He felt like crying, such terrible things had happened. Would have been better if he'd just had a fist fight with George Peach, and taken a beating.

That would have been a hell of a lot better than this. This was all right if you were tough. If you weren't tough, it was terrible.

He'd died and gone down to hell, is probably what had happened. George had probably shot him dead in the Black Ace, and everything else was hell.

Lee leaned over his saddle-bow and tried to vomit again. Just trying hurt his side something fierce, but he was so sick he certainly needed to vomit. "Let it out of you, dear . . ." his mother would say. "Let all the nastiness out, I won't mind." And hold his head, hold his forehead in her cool hand.

A man called a halt.

Logan.

And in jolts, yanking on lead—sidling this way and that—Lee's sweating horse pulled up, throwing him forward against the saddle-bow.

A rider coming by. "Say, Kid—how goes it?"

Lee took a while to get his breath. "O.K." he said.

"Now, there's the dandy," said Harvey Logan, out of the dark. "That's a fine fellow. You know, Mister Moon has taken two bullets to your one—and the pair of you riding along like cavalry!"

Lee felt ashamed to be pleased at this praise, right after thinking about his mother.

"We're getting down here, Kid," Logan said. "Willie, climb on down—and take a rest for the horses." He turned and rode on past. "Matt," Lee heard a horse's hoof strike stone, "shuck 'em off an' rub 'em down; we'll hold here an hour or so."

"I'll do her!" A young voice, out of the dark.

Lee was just glad to be sitting still. No motion of a train, no motion of a horse. Just sitting still . . .

They made cold camp, and stayed in it until the first light of dawn. By that light, Millie took Lee's vest and shirt off to the morning chill, cleaned his rifle wound with a bandanna and cold water from a sink in the woods below the camp, and pronounced it not so much.

"If that had caught a rib, Kid," Logan agreed, having strolled over to look, "it would have torn the bone right out of you. As it is, you'll have only a case of the sores, and not even that after a week or two."

Lee craned his neck to see for himself, and saw a narrow blue tunnel running between two of his ribs. Slow blood welled from it in spots.

"It'll be hurting you for a while," the woman said, tore a long white strip of linen from her petticoat—showing a fine ankle when she did—and bound Lee's chest with it, clear around.

"Enough playing with that handsome boy, there," Logan said to her, pleasantly. "Go tend Moon." At this exchange, Lee saw Matt Serle grinning at him from across the space where a fire would have been, if they'd dared have one.

"They'll be coming after us hot and heavy," Logan

had said. "And don't think they won't. Silliness and stubbornness cost some people their lives back there, and will inflame the authorities."

Lee had thought that was a mild way to put it. It had been a damned massacre, was what it had been! And the law of every State and Territory within a thousand miles would be after them like fury.

So there'd been no fire. And there would be another two hundred miles of riding to the hideout, wherever the devil that might be . . .

Lee did not return Matt Serles' grin. Serles seemed all right, a tall gawk of a fellow, and about Lee's age, with a beginning beard and mustache on him that looked plumb ridiculous.

Good enough for a horse-holder, maybe. Maybe not good enough to rob a train and see more killings than he had fingers on a hand! Lee had to smile at himself for thinking in that way—playing the fierce dasher, now that the woman had said he wasn't going to die of the wound . . . now that they were away clean, and not lying hogtied by a hanging tree, waiting on a posse's pleasure.

A fierce young fellow for certain—for right this minute.

He looked up at Matt, and winked at him. Fellow was lucky to have only held the horses. Lucky.

Lee saw his possibles sack in a heap of goods off the pack horse. The mailbag was there as well. He had a sudden chill at the notion he might have lost that gold, fainting away as he had on that platform, with the guns going off. If that gold had been lost, and it his fault, only God knew what Harvey Logan would have done to him.

Millie—Lee wondered what her last name was—

was tending the Indian, now, had his shirt off as she'd done with Lee. The man had a body like a statue's in one of Professor Rile's picture books. All carved of redwood. There'd been a blacksmith named Harney in Cree, the most powerful man thereabouts. The Indian, Moon, could have broken Harney's back, and no doubt of that at all.

There was a small black bullet hole high up on the giant's naked shoulder. A little blood oozed from it. Low down on his side, his right side, was another wound, and that bled freely as Millie What's-her-name dabbed at it.

Fellow had taken two solid hits, and appeared to make nothing of them. He sat, enduring the woman's hands as if she were not there at all, staring away to the light of dawn over the mountains to the west. He still wore his fine gray plug hat, in the Indian manner, set straight and square on his head.

Logan came strolling by—appeared too restless to sit at his ease, even after hours in the saddle, and all that had gone before. His natty suit was black and stiff with blood. Lee was curious enough to look to see where Logan carried that sudden Colt's of his—and saw, he thought, the slight bulge of a neat holster high on Logan's right side, under his dirty suit coat.

He had no notion where Logan carried that jack-knife.

Logan hunkered down beside him, chewing steadily on a stem of grass. "That big boy over there say he was going to deal hard with you?" he said.

"He bumped into my arm walking down the aisle," Lee said, "and got all tough about it." With some shamed hope that Logan would settle that matter at once.

"Well," Logan said, chewing the shred of grass up and swallowing it, "he'll likely try it on, then, sometime when I'm not about. I was you—I'd shoot for the head."

Lee managed a grin to match Logan's pleasant one. No use showing you'd wished he'd played daddy. But Logan kept smiling at him, not fooled at all.

"Moon's too useful a man for me to kill," he said, patted Lee on the shoulder, and stood to go off pacing again. "Did you know that red nig's an eastern college man?" he said. "That fellow went two years to Brown University, played their football there." And he strolled away, leaving Lee to examine the first eastern college man he'd ever seen, to know of.

Fellow looked as though he'd rather eat a cavalry sergeant's heart, then parse Julius Caesar.

Lee saw that Logan had gone over to the mailbag, was dumping it out, then opening the small gold sacks, one by one. He unknotted the rawhide tie at each sack-mouth, spread it open, and began to pour the contents out onto a horse blanket.

The gold coins shone in the rising sun.

Logan counted them all. It took some time. Then he put the coins away, and packed the gold sacks back into the mail-bag.

He looked up, smiling. "Thirty-seven thousand dollars, boys!" He stood up and dusted off his blood-stiffened trousers. "Thirty-seven son-of-a-bitchin' thousand dollars. It is the best score that I have ever made since Cassidy skedaddled! And by God, even then we only had just one bigger!"

He looked around at them. "That'll be seven

thousand gold dollars for each of us, and then some."

Lee was surprised at that one—had assumed Logan would take the lion's share, once he'd started counting over there. Truth was, before that, Lee hadn't thought about getting any money out of the robbery. The robbery hadn't seemed to be *about* money, somehow.

Now, though, he saw that it was. Logan might enjoy the doing of the thing, but he liked the pay as well. And only took a regular share. Lee supposed that was because Logan was, in a way, a fair man.

Or had learned, perhaps, that it kept the stooling down, to split even.

Seven thousand dollars. *Seven thousand dollars.*

The price of a little scrub ranch, and some stock, too.

The price of a trip to London, England—or to Paris, France—and a stay there as long as you pleased.

The price of a good education back east—and some left over.

Damn! He was a robber and a thief for sure.

CHAPTER SEVEN

THEY HAD ridden for six more days. South.

"Utah's the ticket," Logan had said—and they rode that way, through mountains and badland, over a desert severe enough to kill two of their horses.

They'd changed horses three times. At a mountain farm, where a silent farmer had taken ten gold coins, and then led out their mounts, grained and ready; at a hard-scrabble ranch in the Little Sawtooths; a Mormon's crossroad store in the middle of the night. The Mormon had taken his ten coins, led them out to his warehouse out back, and paraded out the stock—good, sturdy mounts.

Then he'd asked for a hundred dollars, additional.

Logan, looking quite small in the dark of the moon, had paused in his unsaddling and saddling, turned, and stared at the man.

He stared for a while, and said nothing.

Finally, the Mormon said, "I was only funnin'." And Logan had gone back to his saddling.

In all that riding—the hardest Lee had ever done; stock raising and tending was nothing to it—they had seen two posses. The first in the Little Sawtooths.

The second, and larger—twenty men, at least—in the desert two days later.

"That god-damned telegraph," Logan had said, when they'd spotted the second. "Those cowardly sheriffs all act in concert against a man, and ride routes with a dozen and more guns behind them."

Lee felt they were lucky not to have seen a third sheriff riding, or been seen by him. The rancher at the second change had told them the whole country was out against them, and a reward of five thousand dollars on every head. *A certain Duschied, a tall Indian buck in white's clothing, a lady—perhaps captive, perhaps not—a youthful gunman, known as the Idaho Kid.*

Five thousand dollars on every head.

On the afternoon of the seventh day since they robbed the express on the Western, they rode down into a steep pass Logan called "Pass Placer;" said an old man used to pan the stream that cut the pass, which creek ran pretty high in spring.

Now, the creek, unnamed, was running high, and the pass, a wide ravine, really, running down the mountain slopes for four or five miles, was blooming with wildflower color, all marked along drifts of rose-red stone.

The grasses were up as well, and the tired horses mouthed their bits, and would keep their heads down to graze though a rider yanked and cursed all he would.

"Now, this," Logan had said, turned in his saddle so they all could hear him, "this pass, is where we hole up. There's a line shack and stabling along a ways, and a creek for water just past it. We're riding on Three-Spot land right now, and that land belongs to a man owes me an old favor." Tired of talking back over his shoulder, Logan had pulled up and waited for them to ride up to him.

"Owes me, as I say—but he doesn't owe you. So, the bunch of you will stay out here and whittle. And when you get tired of that, why whittle some more, because you, none of you, are riding out of this pass for two months, at the inside."

No one had anything to say to that, not even the Indian. Lee wondered—as much as his aching butt and the pain in his side, would let him wonder about anything but getting off his horse and never getting on another—he wondered how Logan kept control of that odd and ferocious giant. Lee supposed that Logan could kill the big man, if push came to shove, and it was gun speed that counted, though it would have to be head shots for sure, as Logan had said. The mystery was, what kept the big Indian from pushing—from shoving, if it came to that? As Lee well knew, Mister Moon was mighty poor at temper keeping.

He supposed that, like the owner of this Three-Spot ranch, the Indian owed Harvey Logan something, and was keeping his white-hating screwed down tight, to pay that debt off.

No mystery why the woman was here, and would stay and not fuss about it. No mystery except the mystery all women made of their attachments.

Twice, on the long, punishing ride down, Logan had taken her off into the brush. The first time, after a while, Lee'd heard her moaning off in the night. Then she'd shouted something, drawn in her breath and shouted again.

When Logan had brought her back to the camp, she was stumbling, the dirty white hem of her petticoat spotted with blood.

The second time he'd taken off, she'd made no sounds, though when he brought her back, she looked beaten.

That night, Lee had had trouble sleeping, and had to practice self abuse.

As for Matt Serles, Lee supposed he do just what Logan told him—and pronto.

As for Lee Morgan—the same. He might, he supposed, take his cut of the gold—Logan left it in a wooden box under the cabin floorboards, for all to know—and fork a horse and head out. But Lee had the feeling, and had heard tales of the man to support it, that Logan was a poor forgetter, and no forgiver at all.

If, by running out early, before the heat of the chase had cooled, Lee caused Logan even inconvenience, he had no doubt that Logan would begin a chase, a hunt of his own, with Lee Morgan marked.

So—there'd been no objection to a long stay into the summer, deep in the pass. No objection then, but maybe some restlessness now, a month into the wait.

No Three-Spot drovers came this way—not mavericking, not riding fence. Not a single strange rider came single-footing up Pass Placer. Sometimes, every few days, Logan would saddle-up, mount-up, and ride. He never told them where, or for how long. And nobody asked him.

Five long weeks in the pass had given Lee all the time he needed to knit up, and then some. The wound along his left side had swollen, full of blood and pus—then been broken, when one day, Millie Avery had pressed it. She'd been doing a bandage on it, not liked its look, and told Lee to hold still. He'd been happy enough to do it, enjoying as he did the touch of her hands on him. It was a toss-up, whether the pain of the wound, more than just pain, too, toward the end of the long ride, had not been worth it to have her looking at him, and stroking at his side, and cleaning the hurt gently with yellow soap and warm water.

In the long, empty, warm, early summer days, getting his shot wound cleaned and tended had become an important event in Lee's day. Enjoyable, and personal.

There was not much else to do—not much else to be done.

"Hold still," Millie had said to him on this occasion —made all the nicer by their being along alone in the line-shack. Logan and Millie Avery slept there. Lee, Matt Serles, and Mister Moon slept in the lean-to stable—no hardship in this fine weather.

"Hold still," she'd said, her bright, hazel eyes narrowed, staring at the injury. "There's too much bad matter in there," she'd said, reached out, put her fingers on the swelling—and not suddenly, but slowly, began to squeeze, gathering the swelling, the inflammation up between her fingers, and squeezing that harder and harder.

Lee had cried out at the agony of it. It felt as if she were cutting at him with a knife. The pain went lancing into him as deep as his lungs.

He'd cried out and tried to wrench away, but she'd crushed the wound between her fingers like a woman wringing out a rag—and in that new and special agony, Lee had nearly fainted away—and with a small ticking sound, something had burst under her hands, and dark blood richly streaked with yellow ran down her wrist.

She'd stared down at that, with a sleepy look in her eyes, then sighed and got up to get a basin of fresh water. "All that is out, now," she said. "Now, I'll clean you up." And had done so, gentle as a mother.

Long, easy, warm days—and, give Millie Avery credit, no more pain from the side wound, either. The Indian had never seemed bothered by his bullet holes, one way or another. Lee supposed she'd doctored them and cured them.

No trouble with the Indian, but no sign the savage had forgiven Lee for that very slight offense. Come to that, if insult was in the air, it was the Indian had run into Lee's arm, and not the other way round.

Mister Moon got up out of his soogins at dawn, or a little before, walked out into the corral yard in his Union suit, hunkered down and prayed—or sang some kind of song that Lee supposed meant the same thing.

"Moon's an Iroquois Injun," Matt Serles said, one morning when they were both wakened by the Indian's singing. "From up in New York State."

Moon was the first old-timer eastern Indian that Lee had seen and seeing Moon, he wondered how the pilgrims had ever got set back there at all.

Lee expected the Indian to keep his silence, along with his grudge—a grudge maybe he didn't care to exercise on Logan—but that didn't happen. Moon was happy enough—or willing enough—to speak to Lee, though Lee didn't understand much of what the big man said, this being what the professor had called "tags and nonsense," in Greek and Latin. But when he wasn't speaking in those languages—a sure sign of a half-arsed education, according to Riles—he made perfect sense, and spoke to Lee in a cordial way, as if he hadn't promised to have his arm off, cook it, and make him eat it.

Moon and Serles and Lee had been out in the corral currying the horses—they still had their last bunch, that the tricky Mormon had sold to them—when, out of the blue, Moon began to speak of horses—commencing with "*Equis*" this and that, then shifting to English.

"Horses," he'd said, brushing away at a dancy pinto named Jake. "Horses—used to be much smaller. Read Morganthau, read LeMaitre, read Darwin. Horses may have been small as foxes, many thousand of years ago. Perhaps a million years ago . . ." It was the giant's notion of conversation, and Lee always tried to fall in with it, hoping to ease the Indian's grudge. It was a shaming thing to do, but he did it.

"Now, that's interesting," Lee said on that occasion. "Small as foxes . . ."

"Easy to ride," Serles said, "but you'd have to change off mighty frequent." Serles was a good-natured young fool.

"I wonder," Lee said, intending to show he'd had something of an education himself, even if he hadn't been at Brown College. "I wonder if Darwin explains how they got bigger . . . in his theory, I mean."

The Indian had given Lee an impenetrable look. "Darwin's theory is *about* why the horse got bigger!" he said, cleaning his gelding's dick-sheath.

"Little as foxes, huh?" Serle said, not having

digested that notion quite yet. "Is that them foxes in the grapes?"

Lee and the Indian exchanged a look, then, of the knowledgable as opposed to be benighted.

"That's the Bible," Lee said. "We're talking about Mister Darwin's new science."

"Huh!" Matt said, and commenced to hook out a left fore.

"Conditions," said the Indian, "made matters difficult for the smallest horses. The largest ones therefore did the breeding, and so, in a course of many years, we have today's horse—a uniformly large animal."

"An' not just horses," Matt said, with more than a little daring, referring to Moon's great hulk.

There was a pause after that, then—to Lee's surprise—the Indian laughed, or at least produced a rattling sound that might have passed for a laugh, even though that slash of a mouth barely opened.

When they were sure that it was a laugh the Indian had produced, Lee and Matt Serles joined in, but only for a brief while. Seemed best not to stretch their luck in humor with Mister Moon.

This sort of conversation, then, Mister Moon would occasionally assay. More frequent, though, were stone silences that lasted a day or two. Silences broken only by that singing in the early morning, when he rose.

It took Lee several slow weeks of the Indian's company to realize that his hopes of easing the savage off his mad were in vain. This realization came, not from any fresh instance of the savage's grudge, but simply from a better understanding of him.

Mister Moon did not forget, and he did not forgive,

That the offense had been nothing, and he probably drunk when he took his exception to it, meant not a damn. He had said he'd hack Lee, and force him to eat that hacked portion, and he would certainly do just that, in his own good time, when the notion moved him and an opportunity presented. All the talk of fox-sized horses, and ancient reptiles in the earth, all those quotes of Latin and Greek writing, all lectures on the subsidance of layers of the earth—none of them obscured that promised intention.

Lee asked Logan—just commencing one of his ride-outs—to buy him some forty-four shells for practice, and Logan had said he would, but first he laughed a little.

"Getting ready for the Injun wars, Kid?"

"Just want to keep slick," Lee said, and Logan leaned back in his saddle, and laughed a little more. "Why, Kid," he said, "you're not slick yet!"

And just how un-slick, Logan showed Lee when he got back with a cardboard box full of cartridges bound onto the back of his saddle-skirt with string.

He rode in the late afternoon of the day after he'd ridden out, went into the line-shack to visit with Millie a while, then came out, dressed in denim pants, boots, and a checked shirt—looking like the cowpoker he had been before a killing or two, a robbery or two, and joining the Wild Bunch. "Say—Kid!" He'd seen Lee sitting in a cane-bottom chair tilted against the planks of the stable wall. "Say—Kid, come on and pop some caps!"

Kid Curry wanted to pop caps with Lee Morgan.

Lee got up quick and went to cut out his horse—a bay named Banjo—and saddle up. Odd how a man with a name can do. Kill a bunch of people—murder them, was the truth of it—right before your eyes, and still, if the name was big enough, a man—a young man, anyway—will be happy to be in their company. It occured to Lee he was not being quite the man he wanted to be, jumping up like a darky waiter when Logan snapped his fingers.

Still, jump he did—and saddled his horse in double time, as the cavalry put it, and rode out with Logan, leaving the others behind.

"We'll head on down to a gully," Logan said. He had his Sheriff's Model in its neat holster high on his right hip "where the sound won't carry all that much; no need to play a trumpet for folks—tell 'em that we're here."

It crossed Lee's mind that Logan might have decided to put him down—and so save a share of the gold. But that made no kind of sense. Logan had no need to play the sharper—could kill Lee out of hand any time he chose, back at the cabin or wherever, and none of the others would blink an eye about it.

They rode for almost an hour before Logan found a place that suited him, a deep, narrow arroyo-wash running east to west. "That's the ticket," he said, and rode down into it. Logan favored a big-rumped black, and Lee followed that muscular rear end down a sand slope to a thin run of gravel winding further down. Logan rode the gravel trace deeper into the little canyon, until they came to an easy bend, with red sand walls rising high on either side.

"Good enough," he said, swung off and left the black ground tied while he walked a little further on. Lee climbed down, dropped the bay's reins, and started after him.

"Bring the cartridges, Kid."

Lee went back, untied the string that held them to Logan's saddle-skirt, and then followed on.

He found Logan in an open place—where, years before, some stream had taken a long spring run. Place some thirty feet wide, more than a hundred long. Down almost at the space's end, a dried gray and twisted mesquite stob poked out of the wash's wall.

"See that—there's our mark." He bent and tore the cardboard box open, picked out a smaller box of forty-five shells and emptied it into his trouser pockets. "Get your forty-fours," he said, and stood waiting while Lee dug them out.

"All right, Kid," Logan said, stepping well back of Lee. "You go first."

Lee squared off at the mesquite stob—quite a way down the arroyo. A few yards further than Lee was used to target shoot, was the truth. Still, he was no damn slowpoke on the draw, no matter what Logan thought—and a more than fair shot, too.

He set himself to draw and shoot.

And the back of his head was thumped by a blast of revolver fire. His old gray Stetson jumped off Lee's head like a live thing.

His ears ringing from the explosion, Lee turned his head to see Logan looking at him, amused, his smoking pistol at his side.

"A man ever tells you to 'go first' on anything—look out," Logan said. "A man who *is* a man goes first without it being offered. Now, go pick up your hat, and never let an armed man stand near you and out of your sight."

. . . No damned slowpoke . . . going to show this man a thing or two, was he? Like hell.

Lee swallowed his bile, resolved to remember the lesson, and went and picked up his hat—holed front to back through the crown (and hadn't cleared the top of his head by much, going through, either.)

"Show me your draw," Logan said. "Quick as you can and fire. I don't give a damn if you hit anything."

Lee squared off on the distant stob again, and drew and fired. *Hit the son-of-a-bitch, too!*

Logan paid no attention to the hit. He stood looking at Lee's right hand and arm as if the pistol was still being drawn, instead of that having been done and finished—and in jig-time, too.

Logan didn't say anything, just looked at Lee's arm.

"I suppose I ought to get a holster for the piece—" Lee began, fearing Logan thought he was an ass to draw his revolver from his belt. But Logan just shook his head, and stared some more.

Then he came up and felt Lee's arm—running his strong fingers down the muscles as if he were tracing where they went.

"Kid," he said, after this considerable silence, "you have no need to be so slow." And saw the chagrin on Lee's face and laughed. "Oh," he said, "take that chip off, now! You're quicker than most—most cowpokers would think you were slicker'n glaze ice. But that's because most cowpokers don't know shit from Shinola about shooting an iron."

He stepped off to face Lee. "Look here, watch me," he said, and the revolver was already there, muzzle steady on Lee's right eye.

"I didn't see that," Lee said, and Logan made an impatient face. "*Watch* me, then, damn it," he said, and tucked the short-barreled revolver back up into its holster high on his hip.

"Can I call it?"

"You been reading penny-dreadfuls, Kid?" Logan shook his head. "First man to draw, calls it," he said, and the pistol was out and beaded unmoving as a stone on Lee's other eye. But that time, Lee saw him do it.

Logan had drawn the revolver the way another man might whisk a handkerchief out a back pocket, that sort of swift and weightless snatching motion.

A strong arm, and a light gun, he thought—and then said it aloud.

"That's the dandy!" Logan said. "A strong arm, and a light gun, and the motion of the arm—more important than any wrist tricks, I can assure you. All that, and twenty years of practice—and most important of all: the willings." He smiled. "A man ain't got the willin's, ain't got nothin'." This last, Logan said in a drover's voice—his own voice, likely, before the years with the Wild Bunch, fine haberdashers and rare whores, the trips to Chicago and New York City.

"Kid," he said. "You've got a fair arm, and it'll get stronger. You carry a heavy revolver—you'll carry a lighter one as you wise up. And I guess you have the willings, though whether you'll keep them, no man can say. I've known good men to run out of sand . . . surprised them . . . surprised everybody, but it happens . . ." He stared at Lee's right arm. "But I'll tell you this—that god-damned arm is not moving right."

He stood facing Lee and made a slow revolver-drawing motion, empty handed.

"Here's what you're doing. You're sticking your elbow way out when you pull. You can't draw fast, doing that, boy. That slows you up like I don't know what. Watch—!" And he demonstrated again. "And I'll tell you how you got that habit, too. You tried for speed before you had your smooth—that's what happened. So now, you draw a gun like a damn Mexican, with your elbow flyin' all over.

"Keep it in!" He bent his right arm, the elbow close to his side. "Keep it in there all during your draw, otherways you're wasting motion, and that's a fact."

He looked annoyed, and demonstrated the draw again.

"Now," he said, "you do it—and you god-damned well had better do it better!"

Lee turned away to face the stob, thought about holding his elbow in close, and drew and shot. Then he stood in the eddying smoke, waiting to hear what Logan would say.

"Now," Logan said, "that was more like it. You were a hair slower that way, what you were doing, but that's all right; you'll speed up good and fast." He demonstated the draw again, still with an empty hand. "You ever see a good prizefighter? They don't flap their elbows around when they hit a man. They set that elbow in close and right behind their fist—and they hit him!"

As if this talking had excited him, Logan suddenly half-turned, drew his revolver with that snappy whisking motion, and fired two shots so fast they sounded like one extra loud one. Two angled branches of the distant mesquite stump vanished in splinters.

"You shoot well enough for now," Logan said, "but not well enough to back me in a fight—so don't think it. Can you hit with your left hand?" And with that question, Lee saw the revolver now rested in Logan's left. The man had a marvelous way of moving that pistol.

"Not too well."

Logan mimicked him. " *'Not too well!'* " It'll sure sure be not too well if you get hurt in your right during a shooting fray . . . *'Not too well.'* "

That speech, or his shooting, seemed to calm Logan a little, and he proposed a match for speed and hitting. "You stand here by me, Kid, and I'll throw a rock. When it hits—go for your pistol quick as you can. *And keep that god-damned elbow in!*"

He stooped, picked up a stone, and tossed it down the canyon.

As it hit, Lee drew and fired into the echo of Logan's shot. A distant second, that was Kid Idaho.

"You think I gypped you on that draw, Kid?"

"No."

"That's right, I didn't. We started together, but I got there first. Try again."

And he stopped, found another stone, and threw it. Lee saw it about to hit, about to kick into the sand, drew as it did, and fired into Logan's gunsmoke.

Logan turned on him suddenly, frowning that frown Lee had last seen weeks before. "Are you keeping that . . . your fucking god-damned elbow *in?!*"

"Yes . . . yes, I am . . ." and sounding like a scared calf, saying it. This is a madman . . . wise to keep that in mind . . . And keep the god-damned elbow in!

Logan walked a pace or two to find another rock, came back to where Lee stood—threw the stone casually, half over his shoulder, turned smooth as a dancer, started his draw as Lee did—and beat him by a hand clap. Also blowing a chunk out of the mesquite down the way.

Lee had been second. And Lee had missed his shot.

Still, Logan had noticed something that pleased him. "You're coming up on me," he said, though Lee couldn't have told it. "You're getting that elbow in where it belongs."

He looked at Lee, quite pleased. "You may do," he said. "You may do." And he did a remarkable thing. Finished talking, he slowly spun a full circle, and another and another, shooting, reloading, and shooting again at any angle to the stob he found himself—behind his back, across his belly, full front and from the side. He reloaded faster than Lee had ever seen it done, moving all the while, never standing still. And every single one of his shots struck home—down a distance of forty feet and more.

It was the finest revolver shooting Lee ever expected to see in his life.

When Logan stopped shooting, he was laughing with pleasure. "I'm slick as a whistle, today," he said. And Lee could only nod.

He could forget about ever fighting Logan with a gun. In twenty years, maybe, if he lived and worked at it hard as the devil—and by then of course, Harvey Logan would be old, or, much more likely, dead.

He'd never match the man, and that was that.

For another hour, Logan target-shot with Lee, and they matched draws every load of rounds.

It was strange. As Lee got faster—and he did as he worked out the stiffs of his sore left side, his lack of practice, and as he kept his elbow in on his draw—Logan seemed to get faster still. It was as if there was a thin wall of glass between them—a glass wall of quickness. And try as he would, Lee found that wall always present. He never matched Logan's draw—not once, and, though his shooting got better, he never quite matched Kid Curry's accuracy, either.

The small man was a genius with a pistol. And, Lee wasn't likely to forget, no slouch with a knife, either. He seemed, as well, to have some notion of keeping Lee by him—to ward off back shooters and such, to second him, perhaps, in a less noticeable manner than the giant Indian could.

It was an unfortunate notion, and made Lee long to be gone from Pass Placer. Long gone, and far away. One adventure with Harvey Logan was more than enough adventure, more than enough sheer fright, for any man.

For now, though, he'd the pleasure of shooting alongside the best—and of almost keeping up, his pistol shot always a fractional echo behind, his lead's strike just a bit this side, or that.

For finishers, Logan had tossed a handful of pebbles in the air, drawn, and blown five of them to dust, *crack, crack, crack* . . .

"Well," he said, when that was done. "That's something I can't always do . . . !" And, when Lee got down to start picking up the brass, said, "Let it lie, Kid, let it lie. We can afford it."

On the long ride home, Logan had some other things to say, in the pleased, reflective voice of a man teaching something that he knows better than almost anyone, to an attentive and talented student.

"Always try and surprise a man, Kid—even if it's only a little surprise. That way, he's thinking about the surprise, when he should be thinking about his fight. Say, now, that a man expects you to be coming in the front door of a place, a whorehouse, say, or a saloon. Now, he expects you to be coming in the front—but figures that you *might* sneak in the back. The wise thing for you to do then, is climb in a second floor window, and come down the stairs.

"Never, *never* do exactly what a man expects. Did you see how I pinched that conductor's privates back there, and insulted him? That all kept him very uncertain. You want your man uncertain—and you being certain-sure, all the while . . .

"If you're fighting a man in close, in real close, the first thing is to get lead into him somewhere. Don't even bother to fire an accurate shot. Get the first bullet in, then follow that along. Stitching the fellow right up his buttons, is always useful in a close-in fight . . .

"The law smells fear—they sniff out a scared man, just as a dog does. If you aren't afraid, they hardly notice you . . .

"Most policemen can't shoot. Most deputies can't shoot, either. But when you get a law officer who *can* shoot—a Billy Tilghman, or someone like that, then that is a dangerous man . . .

"The Pinkertons are more trouble than anyone else. They use that damn telegraph night and day . . .

"Cassidy—I suppose he's still alive down there—was a nice man, pleasant to be with. Sundance was a nice fellow, too, but a bit of a loose mouth on him. Tracy is a dangerous man and always was . . . wonderfully good with a rifle . . ."

Harvey Logan kept talking this way all the ride home, telling Lee a good deal he found interesting—and some things he'd rather not have heard. The small man seemed fond of him—or as fond as Logan got. Lee didn't like it. It made him more and more anxious to get out of Pass Placer.

Been in the damn place long enough.

He'd learned how to keep his elbow in when he drew a pistol; learned that a man afraid of dying will do most anything for the chance of staying alive, learned a dozen tricks of saloon fighting and brawling and shooting. And heard more about robberies and killings than he cared to remember.

Even from Logan's say-so—and despite the haul they'd made from the Western—armed robbery began to seem a chancy way of doing. Maybe more chancy, now, than it had been when the frontier had been truly wild, and there'd been no telegraph key at every station on every railroad line.

Lee was tired of it—and despite the pleasures of shooting a revolver with such a master—more than a little tired of Logan. He was sick of being frightened of the man. He wanted a breath of free air. Free of Logan—and free from the threat of the law while he was with Logan.

He wanted out.

Logan had been silent for a short while, no more tales of this and that, advice on this and that—the last had been an advisory on sticking, rather than cutting, in the use of the knife in a fight. "Not in butcher's work, of course, like that fool conductor . . ."

After that, some silence as they rode.

Then, as they rode across the wide pass's floor toward the line-shack and stable, Lee saw smoke coming from the shack's stove pipe. (Millie would be heating that huge iron pot of beans and beef again, for supper). Logan, perhaps reminded by that sight, said: "Bats in her belfry."

"What?"

"Millie," Logan said as they rode. "She's got bats in her belfry."

"Why," Lee said, treading mighty careful, "she seems all right to me."

Logan shook his head. "Nope," he said. "She's crazy as a hatter." He slanted a glance at Lee. "What decent woman, in her right mind, would be coming along with a dangerous dog like me?"

Lee said nothing at all to that.

"She came to see me in jail in Tennessee—they were temperance singers. Her daddy's a Presbyterian minister, you know. But her mother was shanty Irish, and that may explain it. She fell for yours truly like a ton of bricks, helped bust me out, and been with me from then on. Crazy as a hatter."

Lee kept his mouth shut, and congratulated himself for doing it.

"What I want is . . . I want you to keep an eye on that Matt Serles. He is a randy mutt, or I don't know them. And Millie gets odd takings." Logan was quiet for a moment, then repeated, "Odd takings . . ."

As they reached the corral gate, Logan said, "So, I want you to take care of her—see no one takes advantage. The Indian won't, he'd sooner cut a white woman's throat than roger her, so that leaves that mutt, Serles."

"I'll look out for her," Lee said, tired of this ride, and glad it was over. Seemed to him that Millie Avery had more to fear from a rape by Lee Morgan, than by Matt Serles, who was too slow to think of such a thing. Where as *he'd* been dreaming of her for the past weeks, and had a constant big to show for it . . .

"Good for you, Kid," Logan said, not having read his thoughts at all, "you're a square boy." Logan swung down off his horse. "Say," he said, "Mister Moon says you named yourself 'Leslie' to him. That so?"

"I guess I made that name up," Lee said.

"Did you?" Logan said. "I thought you might be some kin to that old-timer shootist killed Frank Pace. You hopped the train in that neck of the woods . . ."

"No," Lee said, and shook his head.

"I see . . ." Logan said. "Fair enough . . ."

They put up their horses, and went their ways 'till suppertime, and Lee began to think how best to get out of Pass Placer, and away from Harvey Logan, and his half-tame Indian, his half-wit hostler, and his fallen half-mad girl.

Three weeks later, in the furnace heat of summer, Lee found Millie Avery swimming in a sink a half mile from the ranch.

He'd been riding roundabout—willing enough to sight a posse and fight it, out of sheer tedium. Would have been well enough if there'd been real work to be done on the place, but there was not. There was nothing to do at all, once he'd shot up all his practice cartridges, and beaten Serles at checkers for the two hundredth time—and been beaten by the Indian the same. Lee could not win one god-damned game from that redskin!

Well over two months, now, in this hole—with Logan scouting off whenever he felt like it for a day or two; probably, Lee thought, getting into some town to pretend he was a drummer or drover, and get his dear game of billiard-pool.

And the rest of them could rot.

Lee'd had enough, and more than enough, and was decided. Logan was gone now, and due back any time. The next leave he took, Lee would take his own, right after. And by God, would take his cut of gold as well. He'd surely earned it.

Riding roundabout in the smothering heat—the sun blazing off red-rock walls all along the pass, planning this and that, Lee heard singing at the sink of the stream, an hundred yards further on.

And pulled Banjo up hard.

They all came down to swim in the sink. From time to time. Logan and Millie sometimes heading out there together. Then, the others stayed away.

Now, from the sound of it, Millie had come out alone. Was down there alone, bathing . . . doing her wash, whatever . . .

The horse seemed to start up again of its own accord, Lee just along for the ride. Damn if he wouldn't see she was all right . . . see nothing threatened her, as he'd been bid . . .

He rode on in, though he knew damn well he shouldn't.

She was singing some Shaker hymn Lee'd heard before, "*Turning, turning* . . ." At a break in the canyon wall, just this side of the sink, Lee pulled his horse up, and dismounted, knowing better than damn well that he shouldn't.

Better than damn well . . .

He walked to the edge of the break, and looked around it.

Millie Avery stood not thirty feet from him, on a strip of red sand beside the muddy water of the sink. She was stark naked, and combing out her long dark red hair to dry in the blaze of the sun. Her clothes lay in a heap up higher on the bank, and droplets of water still sparkled in reflected sunlight on her pale skin.

Lee had seen other women naked—if not many. He had never seen a woman who looked like this.

Millie Avery had long and very slender legs. Legs almost skinny in their slenderness. Lee could see a faint, pale gold down along her shins.

She had a small, soft ass, like a young girl's—and, in front, a dark red puff of fur, like a soft bird's nest between her legs. As she worked at her hair—lifting masses of it to the light and heat, and combing it out again and again—her breasts, large for her slender frame, and so traced with light blue veins that he could make them out from where he watched, shook and swung heavily with the motion of her lifted arms.

She was an extraordinary thing to see—and all naked, out in the open air, in the bright sunlight.

Lee would rather have died right then, than stop looking at her. Would rather have died than turned and mounted and ridden away. The sunlight seemed to burn right down into his head; the heat of it was dancing off the red rock all around him. The whole world looked red and gold.

He walked out and around the edge of stone, and walked toward her as if he were that very train they'd robbed, and like it, ran on tracks.

She looked up at the sound of his boots on sand and gravel, perhaps thinking that Logan had ridden in, come out to her—but when she saw it was Lee, she made no move of surprise. Naked, she stood in the raw sunshine, and watched him walking to her. There was no expression on her face at all.

Then she said, "Good afternoon," and made no move to cover herself, but stood still, her comb in her hand, her hazel eyes bright as jewelry. The Utah sun had browned her face and lower arms and hands. The rest of her was white as milk—she and Logan used to taking their swim baths in the evening—except for the dark bush between her thighs . . . the small red nipples.

"Good afternoon," Lee said, as if it was all in a dream—and walked up to her, and reached out and put his hand on her.

Her skin was cool from the water, and hot from the sun, both at once. Lee put his hands on her fine-boned shoulders, and held her that way for a moment, and she did nothing but look back into his eyes.

He would have had to touch her if she'd been made of molten brass. He took his hands off her shoulders, and put them on her naked breasts.

"Oh," she said, when he did that. And "Oh," again. And stood still and let him do it. Let him gather up the soft, trembling meat of her in each hand—and feel, and gently rub it, and squeeze it, then squeeze it harder, crushing each breast in his hands as she'd squeezed and squeezed the pus out of his bullet wound.

He dug his fingers into her, and left red marks on tender white, made her small nipples slowly swell, puffed with blood from the pressure of his hands.

Slowly, slowly, Millie Avery sagged against him, until she leaned full on him, her eyes open, looking up at him, watching his face as he moved his hands over her, leaving her bruised breasts to slide down the flat belly—and on down to a soft fleece of hair—and past that, to her thighs, polished, smooth, and solid with woman's muscle.

When he brought his right hand up again, she spread her legs for him. Spraddled them as she stood, her knees held wide so that he could get at her. He found her hole lower than he thought it would be—tucked back up between her thighs. There was a slippery spot there, in the fur, and Lee pressed it with a finger, and the finger slowly slid up into a narrow wet, and up into her.

"Oh, gracious," she said to him. "Oh, gracious." And otherwise stood still and silent . . . his finger up inside her, searching into her, in the stickiness, the slickness and heat.

Looking down, Lee saw her narrow, white bare feet, straining up on tiptoes, wide-stanced on the hot red sand.

He reached down with one hand to fumble at his belt, then had to take his other hand away from her, to get it open, to get his trousers pulled down—the Remington falling to the sand and to hell with it. He pulled his underdrawers down then, too, and stood naked in front of her, his cock standing up and out, swollen to bursting.

She stared down at it, and Lee had a need for her to do what the whore, Mary Spots, had done to him —reached up and put his hand at the back of Millie's neck, and then pulled her head down to him, so suddenly that she staggered, and then fell awkwardly to her knees.

He took his cock in his hand, held her head still with the other, and pulled her face against it.

As if she'd been waiting for that force, that insistance, Millie Avery opened her mouth as wide as she could, and put her mouth on his cock with a grunt.

She sucked at it with a sort of desperation—pulling and bucking her head back and forth, her cheeks hollowed as she licked and sucked at him. Her eyes were wide open.

Lee felt himself going—and wouldn't. Not that way.

He caught his breath, and forced her mouth off him, pushed her eager head away.

The woman fell back on the sand, and lay there, looking up at him. She didn't squint in the full glare of the sun, just lay naked in the sand, those full, white breasts sagging a little sideways with their own weight.

As Lee looked down at her, she slowly drew up her knees—then, just as slowly, spread them wide apart, so that she opened there like a book.

It was the first time Lee had seen any woman so clearly—seen how they were made . . . down there. It was a swollen, bright-red slit, opening out, and all in a nest of dark red hair that caught the sunlight in tiny red-wire curls. Her thighs were held so wide Lee saw the sharp ridge of tendon standing on the inside of her thighs; they rose out of white flesh, stood along a line, then sank into her again, just short of the nest of sunlight and wet meat. It seemed as though he could see all the way up inside her, as though, if she wished, Millie Avery could turn herself inside out completely, and be all red, and wet, and slippery soft.

Lee knelt to her—and she reached out with strong sunbrowned hands, gripped him, and pulled him to her.

It was hot, hot and soaked at the opening, and he felt the hair slightly rough around his cock as he put it to her, felt the tip, swollen hard as stone, push in, just the tip . . . with a sticky sound.

She said something in a low voice—talking to herself—let go of his cock, and slowly drew her long, slender legs up along his side—up higher and higher, until, her feet arched, toes pointed up at the sky, she groaned, and he slid all the way into her.

His cock made a wet sound, going in, and Lee, overcome with pleasure, came down on her, gripped her with his hands to hold her, and kissed her on the mouth.

Then he pumped out, slowly. Then drove slowly back into her again. Then out—and she tore her mouth away from his and drew in a gasping breath—and he drove into her again.

She smelled wonderful; there was a glue smell, and a smell like vanilla, and Lee knew he was supposed to take his time—had had enough experience, had heard enough talk to know he was supposed to take his time . . .

But he couldn't.

He wanted everything from her. And he couldn't wait for it—felt that he'd already waited long enough. Weeks and weeks of waiting.

He moved faster, harder—driving into her, driving her into the sand, thrusting into that clinging, gripping oiliness. He heard the wet smack of their meeting, heard the liquid sounds she made when she took it all the way—then almost out, then all the way in.

Lee wanted to kiss her again, but her head was moving from side to side as he fucked her, sand caking in her damp hair.

"Ohhhhoooo . . ." Her mouth was wide open. Her eyes wild as she began to slowly thrash under him—as if his cock were hurting her, hurting her so that she couldn't bear it anymore.

"Oh . . . dear . . ." She tried to draw in a breath. "*Ohhh, dear . . .!* And she rose up under Lee like a bucking mare, and the long slim legs were kicking out at either side.

He felt it coming up out of him, coming out hot, so that it melted him. Coming out . . .

"Ah, Jeeeesus! *Ah, Papaaa!*" She screamed it out, her head thrown back, her eyes staring blind into the sun.

Lee came into her deep—pumping, pumping it into her. He loved her . . . He loved her. It was the greatest pleasure he had ever known.

She lay beside him a little later—they'd gone in the sink naked to wash off, then come back and stretched out on the saddle-blanket from her mare—she lay there staring at him, reaching out to stroke his hair.

Lee was about to say what was on his mind—that he loved her, wanted her to come with him . . .

"I hope Harvey won't mind too much," she said.

For an instant, Lee said nothing. He lay there on the blanket, buck naked, looking at the naked body of the woman he'd loved—and a slow tide of ice came crawling up his back.

"What the hell did you say . . .?" he said.

"I don't think Harvey will mind too much," she said. "He understands a lot about people—"

"Never say you're going to *tell* him for God's sake?!"

She seemed surprised. "I tell Harvey everything," she said. "That was the first thing he taught me."

Lee sat up, feeling strange.

"If you tell him that," he said, "he'll kill the both of us. Now, listen—"

"I tell Harvey everything. He's very different from my father. My father made me keep secrets."

Crazy. She was *crazy*.

Lee tried once more. "Logan will surely kill the two of us if you tell him anything about this! I want you to come—"

"You don't understand Harvey at all," she said. "There's nothing I can't tell Harvey."

Lee's body seemed to move for him, while he was still trying to think of a way to persuade her. His body leaned forward and kissed her on the lips, said: "You're very beautiful, Millie; I'll never forget you." —Then got to his feet, went to its clothes, got dressed, picked up the pistol out of the sand—and ran for its horse, calling back to that naked splendor, "For Christ's sake, don't tell him anything . . .!"

Forked that Banjo—and rode.

And Lee was damn glad to have all that done—and no time wasted.

He spurred the bay hard, lining out for the shack—and his heart was thumping in his chest as if Kid Curry was already coming up behind him.

Lee dismounted running at the shack, pounded up the split-plank steps and inside, and went to the near left corner to pray and haul at the floorboards there. Logan was due to ride in anytime. "Be quick, now—be quick for your life . . .!" It was as if he could hear that voice, his own voice, in his head.

In a rich smell of cooking beans and beef, Lee dug and wrenched at lumber for that gold. Tore the last plank away—yanked open the top of the wooden box, and took just one small heavy sack from the row packed in there. Likely five thousand, not seven, and to hell with it; count that the price of the horse, and the weeks of keep.

He left the shack on the jump—had just put the box top back on, not bothered to replace the lumber—and let the tired bay wander while he ran the hundred yards to the stable for his possibles and any saddle and tack he found.

The gold was heavy in his hand and just fit into a wide vest pocket, sagging the cloth. Lee heard the sound of wood chopping as he ran to the stable. The Indian, cutting firewood.

He snatched up his possibles sack—a two-quart canteen from a nail on the wall—and cleared out, heading for the corral and a mount, and scanning the distant line of the pass wall as he ran, boots pounding on red clay, to see if there was a tiny horse, a tiny rider, already in view.

Nothing. Not yet.

He'd run Banjo all day long, now. Would need a fresh one—the chunky brown, Buster, if he could catch him up . . .

And, for a wonder, Buster didn't shy—stood stock still, in fact, and let Lee put a saddle on him. Everybody's saddle and nobody's saddle; no theft there. Lee threw the blanket, heaved the saddle up, and bent to reach the cinch-strap, draw it under. He was feeling just a little easier. Hell, he was almost out of this damn place!

Just as he tight-hauled the cinch, and buckled it in, Lee heard the corral gate swing shut behind him.

"Do you imagine that you can run from me so easily, you young white devil . . . you evil thing?"

Lee turned from the horse's side—and saw Mister Moon, his great chest bare and running sweat in the sunlight. There was no expression on the big Iroquois' face, except, perhaps, a certain satisfaction. He had the broad ax still held lightly in his hands, from his wood cutting, and no other weapon.

A sudden wave of almost physical sickness struck Lee—it wasn't fair. It wasn't fair! To fear Logan—to be running as hard as he could from that man—and now this . . ."

"Leave me be, Moon. I don't want to kill you."

"But I shall not 'let you be' . . ." the giant said in his dude's accent. "I shall do precisely what I promised you—first, your arm . . ." And he raised the ax, and came for Lee quick as a quarter horse.

There was no more time. Lee drew and shot for the Indian's head.

The Remington missed fire.

Lee heard the grating sound as he cocked quick as

he could for another try—and misfire. Sand. Sand in the action of the piece! The beauty of that bitch had killed him. . . .

He ducked a sweep of the ax that hissed, it came so hard—snatched up his possibles sack from the corral dirt as he ran, tore the sack's tied mouth open, and pulled the backsnake coiling free.

If only this red son-of-a-bitch would give him room . . .!

And the Indian did. Moon, who would certainly have had Lee hacked and dying, if he kept to his rush, now stopped, just for a moment, to consider the whip. It was a fighting man's reasonable response, and it gave Lee a chance to live.

The corral was a big one, thank God, but it was board-sided, with the boards set close together. Too close together for a quick scramble through them, not before Moon would be on him with the ax.

A place to fight then, but no place to run.

The horses—the saddled brown among them—had huddled at the far side, smelling fear, and trouble.

The Indian made up his mind—and rushed. But Lee had had his moment, and used it. The lash of the blacksnake lay straight out behind him on the corral dirt—the weighted handle was cocked over his shoulder.

As Moon came bounding for him, the ax whirled up for that single murderous chopping blow. Lee's arm came down and around. No second chance . . .

The slim black lash—no thicker than a grown man's thumb, and fifteen feet in length—rose from the dirt like a live thing, coiled and uncoiled as it sang through the summer air, curled its length to the very tip of the lash, that tiny weighted tab of pounded tin . . . and struck Mister Moon, with the crack of a rifle shot, at his left eye.

The eye—hit with a blow severe enough to have broken bone—was smashed in its socket like an egg.

And Lee ran to his right—to the Iroquois' blind side—and shook out the coils of his whip again.

The giant had stumbled to a halt at the agony of that wound—and one great hand had risen to touch the bright blossom of blood and milky fluid that had sprouted there on his face. Moon shook his head, and blood spattered around him, droplets shining like rubies on his sweating skin.

He touched the place—did not cry out, or curse Lee, or say anything. He touched it, turned his head slightly to see Lee the better with his right eye—black and glittering as a narrow piece of obsidian—and came for him again, the ax held up and across his chest, handle gripped in both his hands.

Lee saw he meant to catch the whip's lash on that handle—catch it, grip it, and haul it in.

Lee could be butchered comfortably, then. Would be.

The Iroquois came at a run—paying no more attention to an injury that would have had most men fainting, screaming in agony.

There wouldn't be enough time to lay out the lash properly—not back-peddling from that headlong rush.

Lee dug out in a run straight at the man—right for him—the whip coiled and useless in his hand. Ran at him, and, as the giant, surprised, grunted and struck, Lee dove rolling into the big man's legs—slammed into them—and one massive leg, forced backward by Lee's battering weight, slipped in the dirt as the Iroquois tried to recover from his missed ax-swing—and the giant fell hard to his knees.

Lee was up and onto his feet behind the Indian, running out for space to use the whip—and turning, the whiplash whistling, as Mister Moon, his smashed eye running red, climbed to his feet to charge again.

Lee struck with a full swinging motion of his arm—the black, braided leather lash leaped up from the dirt in a rolling coiling curve, curled, and cracked like a splitting board up into the Indian's groin.

Moon stood on tiptoe for an instant, frozen with the agony that must have clamped to him from that blow. But only for an instant. Only for the barest instant. Then—steady on his feet again—he came lumbering through the anguish he was suffering, to hack Lee apart . . . to fulfill his promise.

Lee was more and more frightened—more and more tired, too. The sun seemed always in his eyes; his legs were shaking, he was so tired. He turned to run for just a little more space, a little more time to get set to use the whip again—and slammed into the corral fence.

The Iroquois was on him.

Lee jumped and ducked away and was hit hard across the shoulder by the helve as the ax-head flashed over and split into a fence plank with a thick, chunking sound.

Lee ran and turned—the whip lash coiling out—and had his chance as Mister Moon wrenched and heaved and tore the ax free.

Lee spun half around with the force of his swing, driving the whip handle down and across—then, as the long lash rose gliding up into the air, suddenly, with all his strength, reversed his swing, felt the murderous force spring outward from his aching wrist, run hissing down the coiling whip to send a diminishing loop into the Indian's bleeding face.

The lash struck Moon just below his right eye with a loud, flat, cracking sound, that in a moment or two echoed off the distant rock walls of the pass.

That blow smashed Mister Moon's right cheekbone, and his right eye, driving from its socket, fell out onto the wound, to hang there by a short and bleeding cord of nerve and muscle.

The Indian was struck blind.

"Jumpin' Jesus!" Lee turned to see Matt Serles standing by the corral gate, staring like a squatter rube. "*Jumpin' Jesus!*"

Lee, staggering, his heart still pounding with fear, looked back at Moon, and wished he hadn't.

The giant had put his bright ax down, and stood stock still. As he had before, he slowly put one huge hand up to tenderly feel at his injury. He touched that fearsome wound, and slowly brought his hand back down.

Then, blind and bleeding, the giant stood in the corral dirt and began to sing one of those chanting songs he sang at dawn.

Lee had seen all he wanted to see.

He coiled the whip, and walked to the corral gate, stumbling a little, the Iroquois' song in his ears. Lee stopped at the gate and leaned against it, then he bent over and vomited in the dirt.

"Jesus Christ, Lee," Serles said, watching him, then looking up at the blind man singing in the corral.

Lee straightened up and wiped his mouth. "Listen to me," he said.

"Jesus . . ."

"*Listen* to me, damnit. All hell's going to break loose here in a while—"

"*Goin'* to break loose!"

"Logan," Lee said. "You better just take a horse and ride, Matt. I'm giving you good advice."

"This ain't none of my business," Serles said. "I ain't done nothin' to Logan . . ."

"I gave you good advice," Lee said, too tired to say any more, and he turned and walked back across the corral to where the brown horse, Buster, stood saddled and waiting.

The horse rolled a gentle brown eye as Lee came up to him, but he stood. Lee stuffed the blacksnake back into his possibles sack, tied the sack on behind the saddle, and, with a grunt of effort, climbed aboard.

He felt a hundred years old.

He reined the brown out across the corral, not turning his head to see the Indian, still standing, singing his song.

Lee waved a farewell to Serles as he rode by and out the corral gate. Then he spurred the brown up into a run—lining out to the east.

Shaking the dust, he thought. I'm shaking the dust of this damn place . . .

Just one mile out—not a bit more than that—on a flat, level stretch of scrub gamma grass, Buster, the brown, put his right fore into a gopher hole and broke his leg.

Lee hit the ground hard, lay there for a moment, then sat up and cried. The horse thrashed slightly, whickering at the pain, and Lee pulled the Remington—eared back the hammer, blew sand from the action, and tried to fire it into the horse's head.

The revolver didn't fire.

Lee, still sniffling and sobbing like a child, tried again to knock the sand out of the action, and blew into the revolver's works to dislodge it.

When he tried it again, the weapon worked.

Lee wiped the tears from his eyes, and climbed to his feet. He pulled his bandanna from his back pocket and blew his nose and felt better. He could almost have laughed. Here he was, just whipped the fiercest man he ever saw stone blind, running like a yellow dog from a madman even more dangerous, and Buster steps in a hole and leaves him afoot not a mile from the place.

It was so bad it *was* funny, and Lee surprised himself with a weak chuckle. The chuckle grew into laughter he couldn't stop, laughter which went on and on until his belly hurt, until it eased in a series of grins and sighs . . .

He had to go back for another horse.

And the chances were absolute that Logan would have come home.

And just as absolute, Lee supposed, that that crazy woman had run to tell him what of interest had happened to her day . . .

Kid Curry would be after Lee hot-foot—and he would catch him, too. Dollars to doughnuts.

Lee sighed a last sigh, tried the action of the Remington a time or two more—would have to clean and oil it tonight, if he were alive to clean and oil anything tonight—and then hoisted up his goods, and taking a stone-rough but shorter course back, began to walk down into Pass Placer.

He made it at dusk. And no sign of Kid Curry on the trail. It was possible, after all, Lee supposed, that Millie Avery had had sense enough to keep her mouth shut.

Possible.

He crouched behind a busted-top ant hill, and watched the place. The shack . . . the stable and corral . . .

Not a damn thing moved. And not a sound.

Then, out past the stable, Lee saw horses drifting in a bunch.

Harvey Logan's big-assed black was with them.

But another horse wasn't. A wire-thin gray named Porto. Slow, but a slayer. That gray was gone.

And so was Logan.

Come . . . and gone. All in the hour or so it had taken Lee to ride out, and walk back.

Lee stood up, and weary and footsore from that long, stony hike, went down to the place to have a look.

He went to the corral first, hiking through the red dust to get there. The horses, looking for graze, had grouped just beyond.

The Indian lay dead in the dirt of the corral—looking oddly smaller than he had in life.

He had been shot neatly through the heart—by Logan, Lee had no doubt. But even Logan, for all his talk of head shots at this man, had avoided further damage to that destroyed and agonized head.

Lee walked out to the horses. One he would have

liked—a dappled gray with a fat gut—shifted away from him, so he picked out a roan with good legs, led it to the stable with a loop of the whip, saddled and bridled it, and tied his possibles on behind.

He rode to the shack. Dismounted, climbed the steps, and went in, thinking that, after all, Millie might be there, cooking supper.

The table was set for three, with three tin plates in place. One, Logan's, Lee thought, had been eaten from. In the plate across from that, Millie Avery's severed head rested in a small caked puddle of blood. Her beautiful eyes were closed, and no longer seemed to shine bright hazel through those delicate lids. The poor, mad girl had not known Harvey Logan well enough.

Matt Serles' head was in the third plate. It had fallen on its side in the blood. Poor fool, murdered, likely, for nothing but Logan's imagination, or merely the tendency of violence to keep on.

Lee wanted to bury her, but he couldn't bring himself to stay in the shack any longer, look for the maimed body in there where Logan must have left it.

He went out back, got an armload of kindling—and set it under the edge of the line-shack's front door sill. Then he set fire to the kindling, mounted the roan, and rode away, as the smoke began to rise north.

Logan would find the shot horse—had probably already found it—and would be riding back to try and catch Lee out as he hunted another horse. But Lee still had the jump.

He spurred the roan hard, and the long-legged horse broke into a fine driving gallop. North. Lee would ride north for a day—or most of a day. Then he would turn east. Not to ride to Cree, and the valley of the Rifle River.

To ride to Grover . . . to Spade Bit . . .

To home.

CHAPTER EIGHT

IT TOOK almost three weeks of hard riding, before Lee broke out of the cordillera of the Rockies, and saw the Gunsight Gap country below him.

It had been a rough ride, and the roan had foundered down the fourth day out, broken by the pace. Lee had forked out gold to a hill rancher for a riding horse—a good tough little cow pony named Buddy, and a packer—a not-so-good sway-backed plug. With these two went a fit-out the rancher also sold him—an old Henry rifle, weak-cartridged, but better than no rifle at all, two blankets, some coffee, flour, beans and bacon, a packet of salt, a packet of sugar, and a hand-ax for fire wood—plus a pot, a pan, a fork and a spoon, a tin cup, an old canvas coat, some gun oil, a candle stub, and a box of matches.

Lee had also wanted six back copies of the *Police Gazette*, for trail camp reading, and a razor, in case he had to shave (his beard was still a little light).

The rancher wanted too much money for the copies of the *Police Gazette*, so Lee let them pass.

With all that truck swaying along on the plug trailing lead behind—the rancher had thrown in a mended pack saddle for free—Lee might have had a genuine luxury tour of the plains and foothills, the real hills and peaks of the Rocky mountains.

Except for the need for hurry.

The mortal need.

After the first week, Lee had felt much safer, thinking perhaps that Logan had taken him at his word about not being related to anyone near Parker—certainly not to that "old-timey shootist, who had killed Frank Pace." He thought perhaps Logan had believed that—and anyway, might have lost Lee's certain trail through the rough country he was riding.

The second day of the second week, Lee had paused on the trail—on *his* trail, really, since he was following no old track—to re-mend the mended pack saddle, which was sadly in need of it. He had finished his mending, and was on the trail again—winding the edge of a lofty ridge reaching up into higher mountains—when he looked back.

Down into a ravine, and half a mile back. (It was sizeable country.)

There—a long way off, but trotting along as steady as a railroad watch, was a small man on a big horse. Lee had never seen the horse before.

Logan didn't appear to be doing any tracking, and he wasn't. He was just letting his horse follow the path another horse had taken, and that a horse might be trusted to recognize.

Thereafter, Lee traveled faster, slept lighter, and had worse dreams.

And often, when he woke, he felt the shame of running to an old cripple and a lady for help. And running into a charge for shooting that deputy, as well. He should, he knew, strike out in a different direction—head another way entirely, and try conclusions with Harvey Logan on his own. Perhaps double-back, and see if he could get in a rifle shot to put the man down . . .

He thought of these things, but he didn't do them. Instead, he ran, riding east as if the devil himself was after him.

And the devil was.

After almost three weeks of busting brush, of riding his pony to a frazzle—riding himself to a frazzle as well—Lee rode out of a rock slide pass and onto high ground over Spade Bit land.

He'd have been happy enough to run onto Broken Iron land, or any other of the Grover marks. But it was Spade Bit he saw burned on the haunches of a bunch of grazing horses, and it was the west pasture of Spade Bit he knew by sight, by the lay of the land—almost by the motion of his weary pony over the country.

Glad as he was to see that country at last—frightened as he was at what must still follow him—Lee had trouble staying awake in the saddle. Day after day of grinding riding and dismounting to lead the pony over scree and steep scrub, night after night of cold fireless, high country camps—short nights, too, when every owl hoot, every small branch cracking in the cold woke him, staring and sweating, and Remington cocked in his hand—all this had left him weary as his pony, tired to the bone.

Lee was nodding in his saddle, walking the pony down through high grass in the locust-buzzing bright heat of the summer day, when he felt as well as heard the soft rolling rhythm of hoofbeats.

He came awake at once, dragged the Henry from its shabby scabbard, and levered a round into the receiver.

He saw the rider coming up over a swale toward him, coming at an easy canter. A wrangler—likely a Spade Bit rider. The fellow had no rifle ready.

As the man rode closer, Lee saw that it was someone new . . . must be some man they'd hired on to take his place. Or George Peach's place. Lee felt a sudden sharp regret about that, a bad feeling about himself. Hadn't he said something to George? Something about George not putting a hand on him? He'd preferred to kill George rather than take a beating . . . was about the size of it.

Or had he really been looking for a chance to show his draw . . . ? To show what a fine, deadly fellow he was . . . ?

A fine, deadly fellow . . .

A young yellow dog on the run, was what he'd come to . . .

The wrangler was riding up, now, a new man for sure. Lean fellow, with a neat gray mustache, and hard gray eyes under his Stetson brim. Lee saw he wore a Bisley-model Colt's aslant at his right hip. Fellow looked something of a hard-case—

"Howdy, son," his father said, "You look like something the cat dragged in."

Buckskin Frank Leslie said little more, as he and his son rode on down to headquarters. Mostly, Leslie listened, as the exhausted boy told his story. And a hell of a tale it was. Leslie reflected, somewhat wryly, that it sounded very much like father, like son. The same damned falling into situations of violence—and then more violence from that.

And this situation was likely to get young Lee Morgan killed. If not by the law, for his part in that bloody train robbery, then by Kid Curry, when he caught up—which would be in a day or two, at most.

The boy wouldn't have a prayer against Harvey Logan—had been wise to run. For that matter, Leslie wasn't sure he could handle Harvey Logan, either.

Had been a day, of course, years before, when he would have been pleased to meet a gun of Logan's reputation, just for the pleasure of shooting the fellow's buttons off. But that day was gone. Long gone.

He listened to Lee's hoarse voice, heard about the robbery, the long ride, the shooting lesson—an interesting lesson, Leslie thought. The woman, the whip fight . . . and the long run.

"Damn if you haven't been busy," he said to his son, smiling—and was pleased when the boy managed a smile in return.

"The law is the real trouble in this. They will certainly hunt and hang you, if they find out you were in that robbery. People didn't care for all those murders, I can tell you."

"I only shot that Texican . . . and I *had* to . . ." Tears in his eyes. The boy was about done in.

"I don't doubt it, son." A considerable pleasure to use the word, "son." "But the law won't give a damn about that. Was your name used on that train?"

"No . . . he just called me Kid, the Idaho Kid."

The Idaho Kid. Leslie had trouble keeping his face straight. It appeared that Logan had a sense of humor.

"Well, we'll just keep tight shut about that robbery, and by the way, that deputy you shot is up and around, and will recover. Which doesn't mean you won't have to go up to Boise for a trial, even so. Catherine had spoken to the man—"

"Chook?"

"Yes—and the fellow has allowed it was the heat of the moment, and not a deliberate thing. But there'll be a trial, if you stay in this country. Don't think there won't."

"I . . . I guess I'll be lucky to live long enough for that."

"Leave Harvey Logan to me," Leslie said.

The boy was too proud to let the relief show on his face. Leslie—though in fact he was not at all sure he could handle Kid Curry, figured that he owed his son the try. Owed it to himself, too, and maybe to a lot of other men. People he'd used his gun skills on through the years. All that practice, all the shooting . . . all those killings, might at last come to something worth while . . .

Kid Curry . . . Had heard of him, of course. Everybody had. Meek looking little fellow, but, along with Harry Tracy, one of the truly dangerous men of the old Wild Bunch.

Robbers.

Leslie had never had much to do with robbery—except for one comic bank hold-up when he was a boy. He'd never heard of the Wild Bunch, though, performing such a slaughter as had happened on that train. Doubted Lee was over that, yet. Might never be over it. It sounded—and even more from what Lee had said of the fellow butchering the girl in that fashion—that Harvey Logan had gone the way of many fierce men who'd held the power of life and death over other people for too long a time. Logan had spoiled. He'd rotted like a piece of meat too long in a pan on a back porch.

And still, a great fighting man. And might be—probably was, too fast, too good—too young to be handled by a man fifty years old, however fine a recovery that aging man had made, however leaned-down and muscled-out from a hard summer's working exercise.

And revolver practice, on the sly? Out in the brush where Catherine couldn't hear, to be disturbed?

Well—a few times. Just keeping his hand in.

And if—or when—Logan put him down?

Then would be the time Lee Morgan was proved true—or false. Leslie had a father's notion the boy would ring pure gold.

"I imagine Logan will be here in a day or so," he said to Lee as they rode down the last rise to headquarters. "We'll ask Catherine to go into town and talk to the lawyer, Mister Turley, about your going up to Boise. And we'll send the rest of the men out for a head count; been needing one, anyway. There's no use having one of them shot down over this; be no help against this fellow, anyhow."

"You and me, Dad?" Lee Morgan said, as natural as breathing.

"You and me."

And had one other thing to say to the boy, as well.

"First, I loved and respected your mother. She was a wonderful girl. But I'd killed a marshal, and other men, and it seemed to me I'd mark her worse by staying. And second, Logan's lessons were true enough, but for one thing. Ways and means of killing are many, but still good reasons make a difference. Harvey Logan may have been a good man once, but now he's only a brain-sick dog, and meant to be killed. And if I don't finish him, you see to it that you do."

And he said nothing more about that, then, and made no plans with Lee, once Catherine Dowd, with tears of pleasure in her eyes, had held them both together in her arms.

And in the day that followed, when Charlie Potts and Sid Sefton, Jay Clevenger, Bud Bent, McCorkle the cook and a new man named Sladen had all said their "*Howdy, an' where in hell have you been, boy!*" and Charlie Potts had told Lee what he'd done to cause the quarrel at the Black Ace—when this was done, and the men had ridden out, and Catherine Dowd had spanked off to Grover in the buggy to see lawyer Turley, and to stay the night then with the Nicholsons, then Leslie had a few more words to say, while he and Lee, alone at Spade Bit headquarters except for McCorkle in his kitchen-shack, watched a restless colt pacing in the holding pen.

"The big stallion, the Appaloosa back in Rifle River, *Shokan* . . ."

"He's dead, Dad . . . I'm sorry. Got a bloody flux years ago; and it killed him. Was nothing we could do . . ."

"That happens," Leslie said. "Carrying a different sort of rider, now, I suppose . . ." and said nothing further about that.

"As to Logan, I suppose he's already skulking

about the place," he said. "Go on about your work, boy—and don't be surprised by any theatrics the fellow may present. From what you say, Logan depends upon frightening people before he fights them . . ."

"What makes you think he's already on the place?" Keeping himself from looking around, glancing over his shoulder.

"Oh," his father said, as he strolled toward the house, limping slightly, "because I'd be here, in his place. And the dog didn't come to get its breakfast this morning . . ."

Lee didn't call after him to ask him more . . . to talk to him a longer time. He felt that his father expected him to go about his business, so he did.

He got out the manure fork, and mucked the farrier's shed, which took some doing, since the new man, Sladen, had scouted the job, and left a round ton to pitch. Then, having worked up a fine sweat, and feeling better for it, he went to have a drink of cold buttermilk and a joke with McCorkle, who was watching four pies bake, and was in no mood for chatting.

Lee cut across from there to the stables, shoveled more shit there; then, two stalls cleaned out and tired of doing Sladen's work for him, took down three sets of buggy harness—cracked and dry as a bone—and went out to the well for a dipper of water to soften the saddle soap with, once he'd oiled them.

It was a hot afternoon, and the high mountain sun sent Lee's shadow out before him as he walked, black as pitch. He heard a squeaking sound, he thought, likely the weather vane turning to a hot breeze too high to matter . . .

And, as he walked up to the well, saw, under the cedar-shake roof, the bucket wheel spinning slowly, and the bucket gone.

"Damn it." Some fool had let the bucket drop down the shaft; be a two-hour chore, now, to fish it out. Then Lee noticed the well rope was still in place, as the wheel turned faster and faster—and up out of that pit of darkness slowly rose the head and then the shoulders of Harvey Logan. Then his hauling arms, his travel-stained suit, still fine, and neatly brushed. Finally, his city man's shoes, perched on the well's bucket.

"Well, now, Idaho," he said—and left off hauling on the rope as he stepped neatly to the well's stonework, and down to the ground. "You're a hard boy to catch up to."

Logan looked as agreeable as a bank officer saying yes to a loan with fine collateral. He was wearing no hat, and his hair was nicely combed and lightly oiled, to stay in place.

"I've been peeking at you and that old party—that's old Leslie, is it?—while you've rambled about and sent the drovers and the lady off." He nodded, pleased. "Save a deal of noise, that way. You should have seen poor Matt Serles run about, with me after him like a cat a canary. Old Matt made a power of noise."

Lee felt sick with fear—and wished, *oh, wished*, he'd had the presence of mind to draw on Logan and kill him coming up out of that well.

"Would you like to live a few minutes longer?" Kid Curry said to him. "Hmmm?"

Lee couldn't answer him.

"Tell you what," Logan said. "You lead on to that

cook shack—Cookie didn't leave, did he?—and I'll have a bite to eat, and talk to you about the value of trust and the weakness of women. About the dangers of trespass . . ." He motioned Lee to walk in front of him. "A discussion of these things will be useful, I think, will make you an improved person for the few minutes you will have. I promise you'll die a better man for it," he said, and laughed out loud.

My father, Lee thought. I have to try this madman once we're in that cook shack. I have to try him . . . My father'll hear the shots.

"Unless you'd care to try me, now," Logan said, as if he'd read Lee's thoughts to the word. "I'll kill you now, if you'd prefer . . .?"

Lee kept walking, and didn't answer him.

"Oh, dear," Logan said. "Running out of sand, are we? Scared of dying, are we? But not, I fear, too scared to take advantage of a poor girl with bats in her belfry . . . Say!" he said. "That was neat work with Mister Moon, though—I'll give you that. Samson in Gaza . . ."

Lee walked up the cook shack steps—out of sight of the house. Oh, Christ, out of sight of the house . . . But near enough for the sound of gun shots to carry. Near enough for that . . .

He pushed open the door, saw McCorkle's back at the stove across the room, the long dirty duster he wore while cooking, his sweaty Scotch checkered cap —heard Logan walk in behind him, and started to turn to make his move. For my father, and for old McCorkle, and make it good!

Logan chuckled, in the instant before he turned. "Don't even bother to try it, boy. You're a dead man.

And so is your old-time shootist, and this smelly cookie."

"Oh, I think McCorkle will live to bake another pie . . ." From the stove. And McCorkle's duster and cap turned around, and Buckskin Frank Leslie stood smiling, wearing them, the flap of the duster tucked back to leave the butt off the Bisley Colt's clear. He reached up and tossed the cap aside.

"Well, well," said Logan. "Joke's on me," and turned to face Leslie, smiling. "You certainly have the name, old fellow," he said. "But I doubt you still have the game . . ."

Frank Leslie—tall, lean, with iron-gray hair and iron-gray eyes, stood staring at the small neat man in the fine business suit.

"I imagine," he said, "that men like you, who steal . . . who kill women . . . I imagine there'll be a great many of your kind coming along . . . It seems a shame to me, that I have to dirty my revolver on you. You're a thing better killed with a stick."

Lee never knew—never could recall, to the end of his life—which of the men had drawn first, had started to draw first. But Harvey Logan, his short-barreled pistol in his hand, had fired into a blast that blew apart the front of his fine suit and threw him backward into the long table, the stacked cane-bottom chairs. He went hurtling back, struck them, and fell in a clatter and crash.

Down, Logan drew a whooping, gasping breath, and, clawing at his ruined chest with his free hand, thrashed and staggered to his feet out of the litter, frowning, as small and dark as death.

Lee looked across the room and saw his father

standing still, as if he were listening to something important, the Bisley Colt's still smoking in his hand.

There was a small bright red mark upon the duster at his chest, and that mark grew.

As Lee stared, his father glanced at Logan—struggling upright, steadying his pistol—and smoothly, with a thoughtless ease, slid the Bisley back into its holster.

"You finish the poor man, son," he said.

And Lee drew and fired the Remington as quick as ever he would—keeping his elbow nicely in—and shot Harvey Logan through the head.

For a few minutes, Lee had his father with him still, and sat on the floor of McCorkle's shack, with Buckskin Frank Leslie dying in his arms.

"Daddy . . ." he said, and said it all.

"You take care of Catherine, son," his father said, his voice sounding as strong as it always had. "Take care of her for me."

Lee couldn't say anything, although he tried to say, "yes." So he just nodded.

"—and get those damn pies out of the oven. If they burn, McCorkle will never forgive me . . . said I'd watch them . . ."

He was quiet for a time, then, and Lee sat and held him, and didn't try to talk.

"I suppose . . ." Frank Leslie said, after a while, "that I look smaller, now." He looked up at Lee and tried to smile. "They always looked smaller to me . . ."

Then he said, "*Shokan.*"

And died.